My "Fictional" Lesbian Life

as told by Sue Handley

ISBN13: 978-1-959350-29-3

Set in: Georgia 11pt/Sweet Purple 30/18pt

©The Three Little Sisters
USA/CANADA

Publishers Note

This book was written by transcription taken by Stella Caughell in interviews with the author Sue Handley. The work is published posthumous as a celebration of life. The book features themes and incidents from a bygone era and as such contains language that does not reflect current cultural norms. The events contained within are not to be taken literally as the publisher can not verify or deny any of the facts retold herein.

Acknowledgements

Sue Handley: My deepest thanks to Susan Fowley for suggesting the book in the first place, to Maria Rivers for her encouragement and making me believe I can write by publishing my horoscopes in her magazine, Beau, out of Charleston, South Carolina, and to Stella Caughell for her patience, expertise and editorial brilliance. This book would not exist without any one of them

Stella Caughell: My profound gratitude to Sue Handley for inviting me to write her stories and to my family and loved ones for their understanding and support.

Prologue

As the old saying goes, the apple does not fall far from the tree. But what happens when, through no fault of its own, a little green apple finds itself snuggled up to a pear tree? It is at best awkward. And can be uncomfortable and even incite rebellion. I am an adopted child and a prime example of this. My adoptive parents were well-meaning but stereotypical Midwestern conservative republican Christians. Years later, they even received Christmas cards from "Ronnie and Nancy" the Reagans. Because of their financial situation and because they had lost a son to Rh factor, their names were quite a way down the list of prospective adoptive parents.

They were able to adopt me because I came with an additional restriction imposed by my birth mother. She mandated that she must be allowed to take part in my life – as a friend of the family - with frequent visits and gifts. No one else would take me under those circumstances (open adoption was still unheard of) and so the deal was signed. I was always around my birth family although unaware of their relation to me. My birth mother had two brothers and two sisters. The older brother and sister were known all their lives as "Brother" and "Sissy". The other brother James was her twin and the youngest was Isabelle (often called "Isa-bubble"). My mother Helen (who was 4'10" was known as "little Nell"). All of the children were largely raised in the Masonic Home for Children in Kentucky. Their father died in an auto accident when they were quite young. Their mother placed them there after he died.

I don't know why she placed them in that orphanage, but according to my cousin Paul, she was quite a bitch. She and her mother lived together and practiced the "old religion" they had brought from Wales. The polite term is "wise woman" and for the price of a couple of chickens she was said to be able to rid your yard of moles, your face of pimples, and your bed of an unwanted husband. She was fascinated by psychic phenomenon and taking classes. On a summer evening in early August, she invited the instructor to her home for dinner. The instructor mentioned that he felt the spirit of a great psychic in the room and my grandmother swelled with pride. She was soon deflated when he indicated that my mother was the repository of this ability.

My mother seldom read cards, but was incredibly accurate when she did. But even broke my heart reading cards on one occasion. She read that a girl I had been dating had become engaged to a man. Carol turned red and I turned white and my mother didn't know what was going on. The only interaction I had with my grandmother (if you can call it that) was when a psychic told my grandmother (while my mother was pregnant with me) that she would die the year she saw the baby my mother carried—me).

So my grandmother informed my mother that she and her mother (my great grandmother) were leaving for Arizona. Also, that the two of them would remain until the situation with me was resolved. She (my mother) subsequently told me I was never to enter the state without letting her know so that she could leave, and that is exactly what happened. The policy at the Masonic Home (in the 1960's, 70's) was to release the children at age 16 to go their way (wherever that might be). Aunt Sissy went immediately to Indianapolis.

She got a job in a rundown/upscale basement restaurant called "The Seville"off the circle in the center of town. The restaurant had a fountain and a strolling violinist, and the best frog legs in the state. She worked there from 1926 to 1946. My uncle, "Brother," went to stay with his mother. Two years later, my mother followed Sissy to Indianapolis and also got a job as a waitress, while James joined 'Brother" at the old homestead. The brothers had trouble finding jobs during the depression and decided to follow in the footsteps of folk-heroes/ gangsters Jessie James and Pretty Boy Floyd. Not being well versed in larceny, they grabbed some sort of fake guns and headed for the local bank on foot.

Once there, they told the bank's custom officer, "Hands in the air, this is a robbery!"

This story comes from Uncle Brother's wife Pearl, who couldn't tell it without laughing so hard, she almost messed herself. Both my uncles were sweet, gentle guys—which accounts for what happens next...Some older female customer became hysterical, started screaming and fell into a faint. My uncles dropped their fake weapons and rushed to her aid, fanning her and patting her while reassuring her everything was going to be just fine. Uncle Brother was helping her to a chair and Uncle James was getting her water just as the local law enforcement arrived.

They refused to leave until she assured them she was ok and then they passively (and without handcuffs) followed the deputy to the jail. The next morning, they appeared before the judge, who chewed them out royally. He told them to go home and take care of their mother and put them on probation of sorts. No charges were ever filed.

Uncle Brother, being totally humiliated, decided to "get out of Dodge" and headed for Indianapolis. There he joined the others and lived in adjoining accommodations. Meanwhile, James settled in Louisville and raised a son while working in the racing industry. The state Fair is held in Indianapolis in September. My family attended in 1929, where my mother met a young red headed wing walker who was performing handstands on a bi-wing plane.

They became taken with each other and he did not leave with the Fair, but rather moved in with the rest of the family. By now, Aunt Sissy had married and had her own apartment. Uncle Brother had married Aunt Pearl and she had a young daughter, and they, along with Isabelle, Helen, and her Tennessee boyfriend Clyde, all lived together. Of the whole family, my Aunt Pearl (by marriage) was always my favorite. She was a kick, and adored my family. She thought we were all crazy. She once told me that at any given time, a member of my family would spend two hours sitting and planning an easy way to do something that they could have accomplished in 20 minutes had they just gotten up and done it.

It must be part of my DNA, as I frequently spend a long time inventing things mentally that would make the world a better place. I start carrying out a plan, but then find five other ways I could do it. And wind up not doing anything. Recently a friend of mine told me I was a plotter and a planner. Thinking of Aunt Pearl, I had to laugh. Pearl said that because Clyde could not seem to hold a job, the following July, in 1930, Helen threw him out, only to discover shortly thereafter she was pregnant. When she revealed her condition to her family, she discovered Sissy was also pregnant and expecting her (first, second, third, whatever) child about the same time. It was decided that Sissy would adopt Helen's child. She could raise hers with Helen's as twins—which ran in the family anyway.

A perfect solution that made everyone happy until one slick December evening. The evening Sissy and her husband were involved in a terrible auto accident. He was killed. She lost her baby and her back was broken. The last thing Sissy wanted or was able to do, in her condition, was take on a new baby. The children's shelter home was contacted. In February, some months after Sissy's accident, I was born. Three weeks later, when I was sent off, I became that little green apple that found itself snuggled up to the pear tree... and so it begins...I'm intend to show each milestone as I remember it, except for my birth.

Of necessity the first will be strictly hearsay, since it occurred on the day of my birth. I was born on February 17th 1931 at dawn in the dark of the moon. Which will tell anyone familiar with astrology, that I am a triple Aquarian. I was born in a farm house in Johnson County Indiana. According to my mother, it was a cold clear day. She heard my first cry and saw the sun rise simultaneously. I weighed just under 4 pounds. The doctor said I probably would not live. As a result, they did not see the need to dress me. They simply wrapped me in a blanket, put me in a tomato basket and set me near the stove. At 4'o clock that afternoon the doctor returned. He checked my mother and then said "Is that baby still alive?" He picked me up and I peed on him as he lifted me. My mother said that right then she knew she was in trouble.

Milestone One
Cuckoo Hatchling

My first memory is of feeling vibration and through a window seeing a number of black lines crisscrossing the sky. The mother (the second one) sat beside me making noises to another big person. I had no words to describe what I observed but I remember even now there were concepts in my mind of people known and unknown.

The mother turned to me and said, "Don't tell your father I got a ticket."

I grabbed onto those sounds of her voice for dear life. I felt I must figure out what she meant so I repeated them over and over in my mind. I still hear them as clearly as if we'd been sitting there happened last week. Years went by and I never mentioned it until a visiting friend told my mother he got a ticket on the way to our house.

I was about 5 years old and I blurted out "Mom, I never told Dad you got a ticket!" She turned very white and looked angry and told me she had never gotten a ticket in her life. I said "But Mother, I remember it!" She told me I must have dreamed it and to go outside and play. When I would mention it again in later years she would shut me down still completely denying it.

In 1985, the day after my father's funeral, my mother apologized, saying she had not been a very good mother. She said she was frightened of me as a child because I knew things before they happened. She never understood my lifestyle, and the fact that I remembered a ticket that occurred during a trip to Indianapolis for my 6-week check-up made her nervous. It happened at a spot in Indianapolis known as "Five-points" where the street car cables crisscrossed the sky. We reached for each other, hugged, and cried. And all was forgiven.

Milestone 2

My next clear memory is lying in a crib watching the shadows play on the ceiling. I now know that it was light streaking through tree branches swayed by the wind outside. I heard the footsteps of someone coming to me and knew it was the mother. So I lay very still and kept my eyes closed. I did not want her to pick me up. I felt uncomfortable around her. Then, a very loud noise sounded and the ceiling turned red. I felt very excited, stood, and started jumping up and down yelling "Daddy! Daddy! Daddy!"

My father drove a Mobil Gas oil truck and he parked under my window. It was his footsteps I heard and he came and picked me up and made happy sounds in my ear. His clothes were rough and he smelled of oil and gas, but I felt safe, comfortable, and loved.

My next recollection concerns my mother's need for a nap. When I was about three years old, she insisted I lie down on the bed with her every afternoon. I soon learned that fussing only resulted in me getting scolded. However, if I was very still she went quickly to sleep. When she started making funny noises through her nose, I quietly slipped off the bed and tiptoed out the back door. Then I climbed a fence. I had learned that when it swayed I could swing my leg over on the down swing and slip right over, toddle across the sheep pasture, climb two more fences, and come to the home of my playmate (and sometime baby sitter) Virginia. I stayed there till around five o'clock when the mother came to get me.

I loved it at the babysitters because Virginia's mother gave me fried mush, rat cheese (cheddar) and homemade cider to drink. I got to play with her pet skunk, "Rosebud" that her brother brought home as a baby and tamed. It did not spray us because he was tame, but he had not been de-scented. Obviously he still had quite a strong odor so the mother made me run up the road ahead of her and strip my clothes off in the back yard, where she bathed me before she would let me in the house. That scent is hard to defeat so she often poured tomato juice all over me. I thought the process was fun, and my father laughed hard, but the mother was silent the rest of the day.

Milestone 3

When I was a kid everyone's favorite child star was Shirley Temple. Besides seeing her movies, you could buy almost any item for a child with the star's name on it. Dresses, shoes, underwear, dolls, books, coloring books, and hair ribbons for example. She was a little older than me but she was portrayed younger in film. My mother seemed to be only one buying me dresses, t-strap sandals, and hair ribbons. She wrapped my naturally curly hair in rags at night. So, in the morning when she removed the rags, my head was covered with a multitude of curls just like Shirley Temple.

One Sunday in spring, she dressed me up and paraded me off to church. All the women there oohed and ahh'd and told me how cute I was and how I looked just like Shirley Temple. I was not a "girly" girl and I was boiling with anger over their treatment. I did not want to look like Shirley Temple! I wanted to be me! It had been raining and as we walked outside I spied a puddle on the sidewalk. Without a moment's hesitation I ran jumping gleefully up and down in the middle of it. I learned a new word: mortified. My mother said she was mortified. She applied this word to me frequently thereafter.

Another thing that bothered my mother a great deal was that I always seemed to know when other people were coming to visit (before anyone else knew). One time I ran in the house and told my mother I wanted milk with my chocolate chip cookies. When she said she didn't have any, I told her I meant the ones Aunt Shirley was bringing. Before she could finish telling me that my Aunt Shirley was not coming, the car pulled up and my Aunt and cousin popped out with a plate full of chocolate chip cookies. My mother turned white around the mouth and looked like she was going to throw up. I couldn't understand why, the cookies smelled wonderful. She must have thought she had been given a changeling.

Milestone 4

It was a lovely spring day with soft breezes blowing. I was spending the afternoon with a friend who lived across the fields in the other direction. Her name was Margarite and she was 12 years old. And though I was only 7, we were close friends. That afternoon we had gone to a small hill next to a stream to eat the peppermint that grew there. The grass was long and soft and bent over from the little breezes. Suddenly a night crawler appeared, crawling along the top of the grass. It was a bright sunny day so I knew it was lost and seriously in trouble. Night crawlers have that name for good reason. Calmly Margarite picked him up and dug a small hole in the ground.

She deposited him in the hole and gently covered him with loose dirt and grass. I was in awe. That was the kindest act I had ever witnessed. It's easy to be nice to kittens or to put a little bird back in its nest, but to extend one's kindness even to a worm was beyond my understanding. I was smitten. I immediately asked her to marry me when we grew up. She laughed and hugged me and told me that I would have to marry a boy – that girls did not marry girls. I told her no way. I thought boys were nasty.

Milestone 5

On December 7, 1941, just before my eleventh birthday, Japan attacked Pearl Harbor. I clearly remember walking down the road toward Virginia's, the sound of my mother's crying and my father's swearing ringing in my ears. The area was full of construction workers building Camp Atterbury, a new Airforce base a few miles south of town. Everyone was singing "Goodbye Dear, I'll Be Back In A Year" (a song popular at the time). The "year" became "the duration". I told myself "This is it. Childhood is over." Everything from then on had to do with the war effort. Food was rationed and so was gas, mother started donating blood and driving an ambulance for Atterbury.

When she wasn't driving the ambulance, she worked for my grandfather (who was the county assessor). As soon as I could, in the spring I got a job "dropping" and "setting" tomato plants. It was hard work - chopping holes, dropping the plants in, and covering them (each plant one step apart). I worked for 10 hours a day for Io cents an hour. By the time it was done I was sunburned, sore, and 10 dollars richer. I missed quite a bit of school as most farm kids (my age and older) did during this time.

It was fine with the teachers. It was for the war effort and most of the young men who would have worked in the fields were already off in army camps. The fields, farms, and factories, were "manned" by women, children, and disabled or aged men. Considering the fact that my father drove a fuel oil truck, one would think that we had access to all the gas and oil we wanted. However, my father, feeling guilty (as he was a bit too old for service), never used a drop of gas he didn't turn in a ration stamp for. He never drove over 35 miles an hour- the speed decreed to conserve gas and rubber tires for the war effort. For the rest of his life he never increased his road speed. During my high school years it drove me crazy when he gave me a ride to town.

The town was bulging with soldiers' wives and their children. And though I was only eleven years old someone recommended me as a baby sitter. My first charge was a 6 month old girl while her mother went swimming. I was good at this and word spread; I soon worked every evening and many afternoons. I was paid 15 cents an hour and 25 cents an hour if there was more than one child. I also picked tomatoes in the late summer. By the time school started, I had saved enough money to pay for all my own school clothes. This pattern repeated until I was 12 and was able to get a work permit. That allowed me to take a job in the local drug store as a "soda jerk". We made sundaes, sodas, and waited on tables.

My pay increased to 30 cents an hour. During late August and early September, I went to work at the local canning factory. It was hot, humid, and exhausting work, but it paid a big 39 cents an hour... I was in "hog heaven." I bought my own clothes and a Hollywood bed and matching dresser. No more sleeping on the sofa. Our house only had four rooms downstairs: kitchen, living room, dining room, and my parent's bedroom. Somehow I convinced my parents to give me their bedroom and convert the dining room into a bedroom for them.

The bedroom had the only doors in the house. They were double French doors and I had to agree to keep them open in the daytime—which meant that my room had to be kept perfect all the time. I resented it bitterly, but I think in the long run it helped shape me into a "neatnick." Also during that time I joined the civil air patrol. We learned to send and receive Morse code, take off in a plane and read the cockpit dials. The instructor never trusted me to try a landing. Every week we flew patrol in an antiquated PT-17. The plane was so beat up that the wings were patched with pieces of feed sack.

It was an open cockpit, and I sat in the front seat. Don Maulindore (the pilot) and I circled Brown County. Largely a state park – wooded rolling hills with little streams running through it. There were three small towns: Little Nashville (the county seat – and an artist's colony), Beanblossom, and Knawbone (Population of 2). In those parts, some kind of chemical reaction takes place when the leaves begin to change.

It turns the sky a pale orchid and is known as "the purple haze." Artists come from all over the world to paint it. Don and I were supposed to be looking for "saboteurs" but we were actually flying fire patrol and taking in the sights. On the way home, he usually insisted on doing two to three barrel rolls with only the lap belt to hold me in. I hung on for dear life with my hands and shoving my feet against the walls. I'm still a sweaty-palms flier.

Milestone 6

I met my first boyfriend, Donny Williams, on one of the few days I managed to get to the local fair instead of babysitting. I was 12 and he was 16. The first thing he did was teach me to smoke. We didn't really "go out" until much later. I would meet him on Saturday night and we'd go to the movies, where my uncle was the manager. One good thing is it only cost 3 cents to get in becuase I had a permanent personal pass from my uncle(?). The bad part was when we sat in the back row to cuddle, my Uncle Bill would come and stand behind us.... Needless to say that put a damper on the cuddling. During this time I was once again working at the drugstore. One afternoon a tall, strong-looking woman in a shirt and tie came in. I remember feeling strange and noticed my hands were shaking.

One of the other waitresses asked her why she was dressed that way. She laughed and said "Oh this is the latest style in slack suits. Have you not heard of Marlene Dietrich?"

Someone said, "You're not from here, are you?"

She said "Oh yes, I am Jean Williams from Nineveh."

I nearly fainted. "Oh my god..." I thought, "Donny's sister!"

She turned and looked at me and said "Oh, and you're "Suzie Q." My face was burning, my knees, shaking... I couldn't understand why I was having such a violent reaction. From that time on any time I was with Don, I would beg him to bring Jean along. I saw Donny off and on for eight years. When we went to movies I made Donny and Jean let me sit in the middle. This continued for the entire eight years I dated him. Jean never gave me a tumble and rarely even talked to me until Donny and my (so called) engagement party. Donny had an older sister who was married with five children. She had a paper route filling machines.

After I met her she picked me up and took me with her on her route. Strangely enough, she wanted to drive with her arm around me. What was even stranger is that I let her. This sister hosted an engagement party for Donny and me with just his family attending. I was 18. It mainly consisted of Donny and his brothers drinking beer in the front room while the older sister, Jean, her girlfriend and I played kissy-face in the kitchen. Both sisters kept asking me if they kissed like Donny. I couldn't really say because Donny and I had rarely kissed, but the girls kept trying. When It was time to go home Donny was reeling from the beer. I refused to ride with him and begged Jean to take me home.

I rushed out and jumped in the car so I would get to sit beside her. She calmly walked to the driver's side, handed her girlfriend in and then climbed in herself. I was devastated I didn't get to sit next to Jean. The next day when Donny called I told him it was all over, and that was the end of the Williams family for me. Years later I heard that Donny had died on the highway while driving drunk. I cannot say I was surprised.

Milestone 7

Because I am an orderly person, I'd prefer to make this narrative chronological, but my life seems to be compartmentalized in nonlinear ways. Some parts seem to be totally unrelated to others, however, when I jump back and forth, I know, eventually we'll reach the destination I intend and all will be clear. My childhood home was located in the country approximately two miles from Franklin, Indiana. Virginia, my playmate/babysitter was the only child close to me and she was 11 years older than me. My mother's best friend, Ruth, had a small grocery store on the west side of Franklin. Her family, including her son, David-Larry, lived across the street from the store. The neighborhood was predominately African American - as was the family who lived next door to the store.

There were two girls in the family: Wilma (my age- The only red-haired, freckled African American I knew), and her older sister Donna. My mother frequently dropped me off at the store when she was going shopping, or running errands. These three, David-Larry , Donna, and Wilma were my bosom buddies. The school, half a block from the store, was an all African American grammar school. We spent hours playing in the schoolyard. One summer afternoon, the good grade I got on my spelling paper, my mother announced she was treating all of us to a Disney movie at the matinee. She paid our way in and gave us each 15 cents for soda and popcorn. As we entered the theatre, David-Larry and I started toward the front row. Wilma and Donna turned and started toward the rear of the theatre.

They explained that because they were African American, they had to sit in the last row. I, my 8 year old sense of justice affronted, said that since my uncle was the manager he would never ask that. We finally convinced them to join us on the front row. A bit later, Wilma nudged me and said to look at the wall. My uncle was leaning against the wall watching us. I smiled and waved and said "Hi, Uncle Bill" He said, "Hi Suzie Q, are you kids having a good time?" We all nodded and said yes, and he turned and walked away. Although I wasn't aware of it, Wilma told me years later that that day marked the end of segregation in the Franklin movie houses. I knew nothing of prejudice or segregation. My grandfather carried mail in that area until he became postmaster. My father serviced many homes in that area with fuel oil and kerosene.

When I was with him on his rounds (which were often) people frequently invited me in for cookies or a piece of pie. Indiana is basketball crazy, and basketball stars are stars - regardless of their color or nationality. The first boy I danced with at a high school sock hop was a basketball star named, Bid Crow. All of his brothers were also basketball stars. His oldest brother was the coach of the Cripus Attucks team of Indianapolis. That team won the state championship four years in a row, led by Oscar Robinson, "The Big O". No one ever asked me what it was like to dance with an African American. Everyone asked me what it was like to dance with a basketball star. In fact, one of my early lovers was a young Creole woman from Los Angeles.

Milestone 8

As a youngster, if I wasn't playing with David-Larry and the girls, I was usually roller-skating at my grandmothers. We lived two miles out in the country and there were no sidewalks. When I was five, my grandfather had given me roller-skates so I would always have something to do when I visited them. The street they lived on ran north-south and was on the extreme west edge of town. There were no cross streets for at least two miles. It felt as though I could skate forever. About four houses up the street lived an old lady to whom my father delivered kerosene, Mrs. Hood.

Often I went with him. When I was skating she would sometimes bring me cookies and lemonade and I sat on the front porch with her. Her house was two story with a window high up overlooking the porch. I often created fantasies around my skating like being in a race or being chased by bad guys. I always felt that someone was watching me skate from that window and I pretended it was my guardian angel. I once asked my father about it and he said that it was Mrs. Hood's daughter Evelyn who had been in a bad accident, did not want to be seen, and I should not mention it to her mother. This fueled my fantasy even more. She became a beautiful, but disfigured heroine who was watching over me to protect me from evil. Once when I was about 14, and babysitting, the kid's mother mentioned that she used to watch me skating up and down in front of my grandmother's. She said she lived across the street at the time and often saw me sitting on Mrs. Hood's porch.

She asked me if I had ever seen Evelyn. When I said no, she said "Thank goodness! That woman was a pervert! Who knows what she would have done if she had been around you." I must have looked surprised because she then said "You've probably never heard of it, but there are women who like to grab other women and kiss them. "If anyone ever acts that way to you, run away immediately! Thank goodness Evelyn killed herself. She was a danger!"

I don't know when I have ever been so angry in my life. That woman was saying evil things about my heroine. I said nothing, but resolved to never baby sit for her again. And I didn't. Not long after that, my father who was always bringing me old toys and dolls from Evelyn's mother, showed up with a red velvet cape. It was chamois lined and beautiful.

My mother looked very upset and said "Bob, you can't give Sue that!"

My father said "Ruth, it's not contagious" Later that afternoon, when we were alone, I asked him about Evelyn. She was his age and they had grown up a few doors away from each other. He said "you would have liked her. She was a tomboy like you and had a pet cow she treated like a dog. She was quite shy and had few friends. When she was a freshman in college, she and another young woman went for a walk in the local park. They were set upon and badly beaten and injured by a gang of hoodlums".

He wasn't sure what happened to the other young woman, but Evelyn was so severely beaten and injured that she never recovered enough to come out of her house much again. He said she was probably in a lot of pain because she finally committed suicide when she was 40. I cried and wanted to take some flowers to her grave. He said that he guessed that we could do that, but that she was buried outside of the cemetery because the local ministers would not let those who committed suicide be buried in the cemetery. I was enraged and swore I would change that, but it was changed without my help sometime in the 1940s.

Years later, after I'd had time to think about it, I realized that Evelyn and her friend were probably raped and I resolved to do something so that people would remember her name. Subsequently, I wrote a story called "The Red Velvet Cape," which will appear in a collection of short stories by the same name.

When I was growing up, the other thing I remember clearly about my father's family was that my grandmother always served Swiss steak on Sunday. She was a sweet lady, but not very bright. She was very much involved in the DAR (or Daughters of the American Revolution), and the WCTU (Women's Christian Temperance Union). Grandmother idolized Carrie Nation who was well-known for attacking, with a hatchet establishments that served alcohol.

On one occasion my Uncle Bill was asked to take a couple of her friends to a meeting of the WCTU. His 2-door Chevy/Pontiac with a front seat that folded up twice to make it easy for people to get in the back seat. When the ladies were seated, there was the crunch of shattering glass when the seat was returned to position and my grandmother got in.

"Whiskey!" one of the ladies screamed, "I smell whiskey!"

"Oh, no", my grandmother scoffed, "that's only Bill's shaving lotion, he always smells that way." ... and sure enough, he did.

Milestone 9

Although I knew I was adopted, I did not know who my mother was, other than another of my mother's interminable bunch of friends whom I was instructed to call "Aunt". I finally found out who she was when I was 10 when my cousin Joann heard her mother discussing how much I was growing up to look like my "Aunt Helen."

She couldn't wait to tell me. I can't understand why I didn't realize it myself—she always bought me wonderful presents at Christmas and birthdays; and, I spent the week with her during the summer at her request and I also spent one or two weekends during the winter. She had even taken me to Louisville to visit with her brother Jim, his family, and her younger sister. They were all fun-loving people. I thought they were the greatest people on earth, but I still didn't realize they were family.

My adoptive mother, with her mother, sisters, and brother were always my close family. Her sister was married to a full-blood Cherokee man. Their daughter Joann, six months my elder, had shiny straight black hair and snapping brown eyes. She was a "girly" girl, who lived in her mother's high heels and always wanted to play "school". I was a tomboy with freckles and a mop of curly red hair. I preferred bare feet and sun suits whenever possible.

I often visited their farm. One day when I was six and Joann was seven, we went out to the barn to see her dad. Her dad had always had a drinking problem and his family bought him a liquor store, thinking they would cure him. When that didn't work, they bought him the farm. We found him in the barn, rolling on the floor, moaning and holding his belly. We ran for Aunt Shirley and I don't remember much of what happened after that except that my mother, his mother, and the doctor were there inside the house with him while Joann and I sat under the Chinaberry tree and listened to him screaming. What I remember next is my maternal grandmother washing my hair and taking me to meet my mother at his funeral. He had taken rat poison while drinking. I think I remember their saying it was an accident/deliberate.

Aunt Shirley and Joann moved in with us. Joann called me "Baby Sue" and constantly tried to make a "girly" girl out of me. I would hide in trees, run back to the creek and pull my pet snake out of my pocket. After 80 years I can still hear her saying "Auntie Ruth, come see what Baby Sue is doing"... she was such a tattle tale. In 1939, her father's parents took her with them on a trip to Washington DC. On the day she returned, she came down with a blazing fever.

The doctor came and then immediately rushed her straight to the James Whitman Riley Children's Hospital in Indianapolis. She had polio. The Sister Kenny treatment for polio was new at that time. The hospital chose to use it on the little girl in the bed next to Joann's who was one of eight children. They were afraid to try it on Joann since she was an only child. Instead they immobilized her legs in casts. She was there for two years; during that time, I was never able to see her.

I was encouraged however, to give her all my favorite books and best toys. Once, I overheard my grandmother tell my aunt that it was too bad Joann got polio instead of me. I felt it was because I was an adopted child. Later I found out that what she thought was that I would have beaten it and Joann was doomed to spend her life in a wheel chair. She was probably right—I have never responded well to being told that I could not do something. During this time, my Aunt Shirley married again and by the time Joann came home from the hospital the family lived in Trafalgar. When we were freshmen in high school they moved to Franklin and I became "the force" behind Joann's wheelchair.

In our high school we were not allowed to have sororities but we did have something that we called "spreads". Spreads were loosely and somewhat self-organized groups of friends who got together before games. There were three main spreads in my school. Judy-Ann's spread Henrietta's spread, and a spread consisting of shy, rejected kids. The five girls from the most affluent families in town comprised one spread, and they invited Joann to join. Since I was always behind her wheelchair, I was naturally included.

I never really felt I was a part of the group, but I couldn't imagine being separated from Joann. It was like being alone in the middle of a crowd who spoke another language. They were all about giggling, boys, and makeup. I was all about basketball, swimming and watching girls with a sense of smothered longing that I couldn't understand. Now it seems I was so dense in those days. Each member of the spread was identified at the games by the flower that they wore. Each group selected a different flower. The thing that held my spread together was our love of singing.

We were invited to sing for the Kiwanis Club, various nursing homes and even a radio show out of Indianapolis once a month. The singing part I loved, but I had very little in common with the girls except for taking care of Joann. In the afternoons, we spent our time in Nick's Candy kitchen, singing our hearts out and learning the new songs on the jukebox. In the evenings I conned my folks out of the car and headed for Columbus Indiana, to meet with my other group of girls that called themselves the bad eight and they soon dubbed me "little niner." I knew the bad eight from scout camp. They were really great friends and all girls who loved the sports and camping that I loved.

Astrology says that Aquarians are born old and get younger as they go along. Although I started managing my life to suit me at age three, in truth I was really a happy camper. Furthermore, I figure that I was either really smart or really lucky to have made it this far. What some consider work, I consider fun. On many early summer mornings when the dew was still on the ground and the sun was barely up, Virginia and I with a bucket and bags would collect a can full of night crawlers and head for the creek.

We strung a trot line that the trout and sunfish couldn't resist and while that was happening we would go through the old abandoned orchard and collect Morel mushrooms.... If we found one an inch or two tall we would leave it and when we came back in an hour it would be six inches or more. Consequently, I called them "magic mushrooms", and found out years later that that phrase meant something completely different! If you know what I mean.

Every summer from the time I was twelve, I would spend a week at summer camp in Columbus Indiana. Each camper had to supply red ration stamps for meat, blue stamps for vegetables and a pound of butter for the week we attended, until such time as the war was over. At age 14 I became a junior counselor and then later a full time counselor. I worked at the camp every year until my junior year in college (except for 1947).

I became close friends with most of the counselors from Columbus. They were my kind of women: into sports, swimming, and hiking, etc. Besides, I was in love with an older counselor from the age of 13. In 1947 she and a friend were flying from Columbus to an airport near my home. When they started to land, the plane hit wires and landed on its back. She died four days later. She was cute, bright, and funny; and I think she cared for me as much as I cared for her. I still mourn her loss.

Milestone 10

No narrative of my early years would be complete without a discussion of magick. As a child I totally believed in fairy tale-esque magic and used it in my daily life. To be honest, I still do. But now, being a typical triple Aquarian, I have had to devise an explanation for it. That is: anyone with the ability to focus their mind sufficiently in a given area can influence the environment. As a child I used it to catch fish, bring butterflies close to me and tame animals. I found my little pet snake, Oscar, sunning on a rock by the creek. I spoke to him softly and concentrated on sending him love.

I laid my hand on the rock and pretty soon, he crawled right into it. I pressed him to my cheek and put him in my pocket and he was my buddy for the rest of the year. When I showed him to my mother, she nearly soiled her drawers! I didn't know she was terrified of snakes. He was only about a foot long and as big around as my thumb. I told my mom that his mouth wasn't big enough to bite her.

She said, "But he's trying to spit venom at me!" she objected. I explained to her that "snakes smell through their tongue and so he was only listening and smelling us, "and besides," I explained, "he doesn't have any venom". My mother was still frightened and made me empty my pockets every time I came in the house.

I fed Oscar dog food and flies, and he slept in a box in the garage that he could have easily escaped from, but he never did until that day that he slipped off to hibernate for the winter. The other wild animal we had was a deer I saw frequently at the creek. One fall day when I saw him, I invited him to come stay with our sheep over the winter so he wouldn't get shot by a hunter. A couple of days later my father came in and announced that we had a "visitor" in the lot. "Come see" Dad said, and sure enough, it was my little deer friend. Hunters driving by would sometimes go very slowly, but they didn't dare shoot, because he kept himself in the middle of the flock. He became very tame. My father even put a two-year-old on his back to have his picture taken.

Come spring, he would bound easily and gracefully over the fences and head back to his home by the creek. He returned each fall for four consecutive years, about the time hunting season opened. My other adventures in animal husbandry were not so... honorable. I relate this story in the sure knowledge that 99% of readers will not believe it. Like many teenagers I was filled with sexual frustration and boredom, and being raised on a farm I saw many examples of animal's sexual activity. On one hot summer afternoon with a storm pending, I was home alone standing in the kitchen staring at the flies covering the screen on the outside. Here, I probably should disclaim that "the devil made me do it." I concentrated on one fly and impelled it to have sex with another fly (of unknown gender) that I chose. It took less than a minute. Flies must be pretty weak minded. Very quickly the two of them flew away with the bottom one making an angry buzzing sound at the one on the top.

I got a mad case of the giggles wondering if I had created a lewd act as I didn't know the sexes of the parties. I tried it again a few more times with total success, though it never lasted more than a couple of seconds. Soon, I became bored and noticed our rooster and half a dozen hens wandering around the backyard.

"Ah ha!" I mused, "If it works for flies, will it work for chickens?" "Let me try. I randomly chose a chicken, concentrated on the rooster and focused a mental picture of them "having at it." It took longer… maybe four or five minutes with him wandering around the chosen hen—she looked perplexed and was pretty annoyed. As soon as she could, she scurried away, looking back at him and clucking it seemed, unhappily.

I repeated this action a few more times feeling very proud of myself and laughing hysterically. Then I was suddenly struck by a wild idea. Among the various fowl in the backyard was a female mallard duck. She and her mate had come to live in our yard year-round a few years earlier. l guess they were tired of migrating. Her mate had been killed in a road accident a few months earlier and since they mate for life she was totally alone. I was pretty sure that sort of thing never happened between chickens and ducks and I didn't even know if it was possible, but I decided to try. Our horny rooster was most obliging. He was probably wondering why he hadn't thought of it himself. But when he jumped "aboard" the poor duck started quacking loudly and flew up as high as she could, trying to shake him off.

He landed ignobly on his rear and wandered around dazedly shaking his head as if wondering, what the hell happened? she flew over the fence, stomped around the yard quacking angrily for about five minutes. She seemed so mad. I laughed until I cried. I laughed till my stomach hurt. I thought it was the funniest thing I had ever seen. At times, I still do. If you think these were coincidences, I have a bridge in Brooklyn I'd like to sell you cheap.

Milestone 11

In winter of 1947 I was waiting tables in a local restaurant. That spring, after having lost Jo, I couldn't face going back to the camp. I knew that I'd see her everywhere. I didn't think I could keep it together, and besides that, I had been chosen to go to "Girls State". Girls State is a 2 week event put on by the American Legion auxiliary where young women finishing their junior year of high school learn political science by electing a governor for their group, etc. It's quite an honor and attendees are usually the two girls from each high school with the highest grade point average.

I think I was chosen however because my mother was a big wheel in the auxiliary because I was only a slightly above average student with mostly B and a few C grades. As a result of all this, I was still waiting tables in the early summer when the carnival came to town. The traveling manager and his wife had dinner in our restaurant every night and usually picked my table. He was an extremely tall and greatly fat man with bushy curly white hair. She was a tiny blonde, barely 5 feet who might have weighed 100 pounds sopping wet. They were a happy, fun, couple, probably in their 50s from Baton Rouge Louisiana.

I loved their drawl and they tipped very well. The carnival was on a "still date" meaning they had no commitment for a fair and just set up in a vacant lot north of town. They invited me to come up and instructed me to tell the people at the gate that I was "with it" because that way they'd let me in free. Boots, the wife, ran a souvenir stand close to the entrance which sold hats, birds, balloons, batons, and the like. Earl D., the husband, and the traveling manager, spent much of his time in the next venue, securing the lots, renting the rooms and greasing the palms of the local cops.

He also painted arrows on telephone poles to point the way to the next lot as most roustabouts and truck drivers could not read. They invited me to work the week of the Fourth of July in Connorsville, Indiana – 80 miles east of our home – and offered to pay my bus ticket, hotel, and all my food as well as send me home with $50 – a pretty sum at the time. Naturally, I agreed. When I told my mother, she said "over my dead body". I clearly remember saying "how do you want it?" Clearly I didn't. I couldn't have been that rude.

Hahaha. After a minute, she looked resigned and said, "I guess I can't stop you". I agreed. That week they set up a second souvenir stand at the back of the lot for me, and they sent a young black man to shadow me and be my protector. They asked me if I would be afraid of him. I said of course not!

He was very sweet and diffident, being from Alabama and not used to flamboyant northern white girls. I think I was the one doing the scaring. At the end of that week, Boots and Bobby D. invited me to stay with them for the rest of that summer. I explained that I couldn't because I was going to Girl's state. Then they asked me to join them when I came back from Girls State, and I agreed. That gave me six weeks and their proposal: bus fare, hotel and food and go home with $500 in my pocket.

I returned to the Carnival in Dixon, Tennessee. We played Dixon, Bristol and Nashville, that I remember; most of the time, a "carny" can't tell you what town they are in because all the lots are set up alike and they don't really care. It's just a matter of following the signs from place to place: setting up on Monday and tearing down on Sunday and then they're off again to the next location. The carnival in those days had a very definite caste system. Owners, managers, "shysters" (that's a lawyer that travels with the show), flat joint operators were all "high class". A flat joint operator is one of the enterprises that surround the Carnival on the outside with the booths forming the exterior wall.

They generally provided some form of gambling entertainment as well. Food handlers, ball and penny pitch and slum operators came next. These offered folks a "prize every time", for example. Bottom of the heap were the freak and floozy shows, the gypsies and the roustabouts. The people on the top layers rarely had anything to do with the people on the bottom. I, of course, as a newbie as well as a rebel, shook things up because I hung out with the gypsy girls on quiet afternoons. Boots, being very sweet and patient, simply shook her head and said, "Be careful, honey, please be careful."

My two friends were Lorita Mattlow, 17; tall and slender with long black hair; gorgeous and dumb as a box of rocks. My other friend was her sister Patsy, 16; about my size, cute as a button and bright as a new day. Patsy once told me that the man who would one day marry Lorita would only be getting a pretty toy, but the man who married her would get a very smart "fireball" that would end up leading the tribe. Gypsy girls, because of their dowries, wound up marrying men 20 to 30 years older than they were. They outlived their husbands substantially and consequently, the leaders of most tribes were women. I'll bet Patsy made it. She made me teach her to read.

One afternoon Patsy asked me to go to a local store and get 3-4 dresses on approval. In 1947, this was still a common practice. One would take clothing home with them on approval, try it on, return what they didn't want and pay for what they kept within a few days. She said she couldn't do it because the stores would not let gypsies take the clothes out.

I laughed and said "Do I really look that stupid?" She laughed, hugged me and said I was "one smart Gadjo".

She then said, "You realize that stealing is not a sin for the Gypsies?" and I asked her, why.

She told me in the days before the crucifixion a gypsy ironmonger became a follower of Jesus. The soldiers came to him to get the spikes to be used in the crucifixion. He, in an attempt to prevent it, managed to cleverly cheat them out of one of the spikes. When the soldiers discovered that they were missing a spike, they simply stabbed Jesus in the side instead of driving a stake through his belly as was usually done.

Then Jesus spoke from the cross absolving all gypsies from the sin of stealing since the old gypsy smith had tried to save him. I don't know if there's a grain of truth in that myth or whether Patsy and Lorita were telling me to schmooze a gadjo. But, all the gypsies seemed to behave as though it was true.

Milestone 12

To fully understand why I was so quick to go with the Carnival, we'll revisit my childhood. As I have previously indicated, I was quite a tomboy. On one occasion my gay uncle, Joe, who worked as a singer in a band called "Woody Herman and the Woodcutters", asked my cousin Joann and I what we wanted for Christmas. I think I was about five years old. Joann asked for a Betsy Wetsy doll, and I asked for a trapeze. My uncle said at the time that he knew right which path I was headed on. I got the trapeze and once installed on my front porch. I became proficient in no time at all hanging by my knees and heels and spinning around the bar. I decided early on that my goal in life was to become a trapeze performer with a circus. I decided I would join the first good circus that came to my area when I was about 16.

I knew they'd take me because by that time, I was quite good. The show I travelled with "L.J. Heth, Inc.", included a free act, The Flying Fishers, a trapeze performing family. Free act people are high caste and therefore I was allowed to befriend them, especially their 17 year old son Danny. Not too friendly as hard as it is to believe; but actually, carnival people were very prudish. It didn't take long for me to con Danny Fisher into taking me up on the trapeze. One sunny afternoon, Danny took me up on the rigging. I thought I was so cool. I climbed the ladder on the outside of the pole like he did and leapt up on the platform.

The platform was a board 18" wide and on either side, almost out of reach, were two trapezes. On the other side, Danny's brother-in-law Rudy (a big strong guy), mounted the 'catch trap". The platform was about 20 feet off the ground and a long net stretched under all the rigging and beyond 12' on each side. Danny explained exactly what to do: Swing out, pump a bit to go higher, and as I swung back he clapped as Rudolph grabbed my ankles and let me go.

Rudy turned me over brought me back and when he clapped again, I was to grab the trapeze and Rudy would let me go. Then as I swung back, Danny would catch me and help me land on the platform until I became confident. Danny demonstrated smooth as silk. I was beyond elated; the entire Flying Fisher family was down below watching while I took the first step towards my dream.

I grabbed the bar, swung out pumped and swung again and Danny clapped. I felt Rudy's hands on my ankles and told myself to let go. It was as if my hands had a mind of their own and no way in hell would they let go. I was chagrined but undaunted. I pumped up and went again Danny clapped, Rudy grabbed and I froze. I tried three times altogether before I gave up trying to swing. I hung there wondering how many hours it would take before my hands let go of their own accord. Before long,

I felt a bump and jerk on my trapeze and looked up to see Danny on the other trapeze holding on to mine. He looked totally disgusted and I felt horrible. Neither one of us spoke. One by one, he peeled the fingers on my right hand off. When he started on the left, my hand gave and I dropped to the net. To retain some dignity, I bounced to the rope and flipped off it the way the performers do. As I walked away I noticed the Fisher Family laughing at me and Danny and he and I ignored each other for the rest of the summer. I felt like a 16 year old wash out and decided that I had better go to college after all because I had no idea what to pursue next.

Milestone 13

My senior year was a whirlwind of activity. It actually started about two weeks before school opened with a trip to a rehab hospital in Cincinnati. The town had raised enough money to send Joann and part of the deal was that she has a helper. The hospital promised to teach paraplegics like Joann the best use of what they could still do. She was there a month, returned home, and decided that her best use was to spend all her time sitting in front of a TV. I accidentally corrected that a couple of years after; I'll explain later.

When school started I was acting in a play, writing for the yearbook, and being an officer for Tri High Y honors society. During this time I also waited tables and baby sat.

We had a little pet dog named Corky who was about 12 years old. He was cute and feisty and I adored him. My mother made him sleep in the basement. She was not much of a pet lover. One of the windows of the basement was on hinges so that coal could be delivered and Corky used it to go in and out at will. One night we heard a big fight outside that window. We had no idea what he was fighting with, but a few days later, he began to act rather strange. My father always carried a large box of books to and from his truck for taking orders, making receipts, etc.

Corky always barked and jumped at the box for fun but now he started biting and grabbing my father's hand and even drew blood a couple of times. Then one evening, in the middle of winter, my mother opened the basement door to go down and shovel coal into the furnace. Corky came bounding up the stairs baring his teeth and as he snapped, his jaws dripped foam. My mother slammed the door just in time. Corky bounced off the door, whimpered, and then it was quiet. Mom made Dad called the vet. She was sure the dog had rabies. The vet came out and they cautiously opened the basement door. Corky came up again hell-bent-for- leather- yammering, barking, and drooling. By this time Dad had managed to nail the window shut and the vet said he would have to stay there till he died.

The brain would be sent to Indianapolis for analysis and if he had rabies, my father would have to undergo the shots. In those days the shots were given in the stomach, were very painful, and made people pretty sick. The house got pretty cold and two days after the vet had been there, I couldn't stand it any longer. I told my folks I was going to the basement to put coal in the furnace. They said I couldn't. I said "Corky loves me, he'd never hurt me, I can do it".

Looking back, I can't help but wonder why on earth they decided to let me try. As I opened the door to the basement, Corky started up the stairs. I yelled "Stop, it's me!" Unbelievably, he did. He turned around, whimpered, and went back to his bed. I went down and shoveled in 3 shovels of coal. As I set the shovel down beside his bed, he suddenly woke up and grabbed my arm. I yelled "No Corky!" and he laid back down. He didn't break the skin.

When I got upstairs the folks asked me if he had touched me and I said absolutely not. They warned me that death by rabies was horrible. I insisted that he hadn't come near me. Just to be sure I washed my hands and scrubbed that place with lava soap. I learned something from the experience. When the school called and said that my son may have touched a rabid bat, I made him get his shots. Having been there and done that, I wasn't going to take his word for it. The shots are not nearly as bad now – a couple injections given in the arm. A sore arm is about the only result.

After I graduated, Bill, my birthmothers' ex-husband, offered to take me to Orlando, Florida to visit her. They had been divorced a few years, but he'd remained nice to me, actually a bit too nice. At the time I thought he was playful and liked to wrestle, but looking back, I realized he was getting pleasure and getting off from it. I went to Florida with him to visit my birthmother. While I was there I worked as a governess for a family that had a place on the lake across from Rollins College.

They had a four-year-old boy named Peter and a two-year-old girl named Carol, and they wanted me to teach the children to swim. Like most lakes in Florida, when you looked across it, all you saw were dozens of little bumps (heads). I was told that 90% of them were turtles. But I couldn't wrap my head around the fact that 10% were not. This lake was known to be the habitat of two alligators: "Ole Joe" four feet long, and "New Joe", a baby and smaller. The other percentage were water snakes. The whole thing scared the crap out of me. The idea of wading out into brackish water, which I could not see, was bad enough, but taking two young, innocent children with me was beyond my comprehension.

The mother had the gall to tell me that a few years before, during a boating accident, Ole Joe had grabbed a two-year-old child and dragged her to the bottom. She was never found. She said that it was "probably a myth" but it was enough to keep me out of the water. Ole Joe had also been known to take any dogs that got close to the edge. The mother also related that Ole Joe was never hunted down because he "was only doing what alligators do". There were a couple of palm trees on their property that leaned at an interesting angle and I wanted to climb one. When I started to climb it, she said: "I wouldn't do that if I were you".

When I asked why, she said, oh, they are dirty. I thought she meant the tree, and so I kept on playing Tarzan, climbing up to the top. I nearly fell and scrambled to get down. Who knew that the tops of palm trees are the nests for the biggest damn cockroaches you have ever seen! One morning I rushed in to get my camera and she asked me what I was doing and I said that I wanted to take a picture of the snake at the garbage can.

She said to get the kids in here and stay here; then she called her husband. She told her husband that I said there was a beautiful snake by the garbage can. I said, "Oh, do you have to kill him he's so pretty? Can't you just chase him away?'

She said that "If he came to the can once, he will come back and if he's as pretty as you say it is, it's a coral snake and extremely poisonous." They wouldn't even let me have the skin to tan, in case it had venom in it. They put him in a burn barrel with some branches and lighter fluid and burned him.That was my last hurrah – I was off to college in just a few weeks

Book Two

Serial Monogamy...

When graduation day actually came I was flabbergasted to find I'd received a "full ride" scholarship to Indiana University. I split my summer between camp counseling and the carnival and in the fall dutifully trudged off to Bloomington Indiana. I was given a room in Smithwood Hall, the same building I had stayed in for Girls' State. My roommate was also a former Girls' Stater, but we did not hit it off at all. She was snippy and snobby and (I believe) jealous of the popularity I had attained at Girls' State. She grumbled and talked to herself when studying. One time she picked up a theme I had just written, read it, and opined, "What garbage" and threw it back down on the desk.

I had been considering ways I could get away with murdering her when the solution to the problem landed on me like a ton of bricks. It was a Sunday afternoon and my parents had come to visit. As we walked up the stairs I called the accepted warning, "Man in the hall." As we reached the top of the stairs, a tall statuesque redhead wearing only underpants and a long tailed shirt came walking around the corner reading a book.

I yelled "man in the hall" again, expecting her to scuttle around the corner and hide, but she didn't miss a beat. She walked straight ahead with all the calm and dignity imagined. She quipped "Well, he's seen me now, big deal".

Suddenly I couldn't breathe. My knees turned to jelly and I was flooded with heat. I felt she was the most beautiful creature I had seen in my life and I was absolutely twitter pated. I have no memory of the rest of my parents' visit except for wanting them to leave so I could follow that amazing woman down the hall. The minute I got the chance I went looking for her and finally found her in the last room on the floor.

I think I said something original, like "Hi".

She said "good grief freshman come in and sit down, you look like you have seen a ghost".

She was chuckling and I think she read me like a book right then. She asked where I lived and I told her all about my bitchy roommate. She asked if I wanted to move down with her and I thought "oh my god, yes, I want to live with her!"

She explained that she had a roommate, but that the woman next door, a friend of hers, was looking for a roommate. Her neighbor's name was Jean and they called her Genius (which she was not). She was under June (my red-headed goddess's) spell as much as I was. I was quite jealous of her.

After I changed rooms, I found there were two other women, plus her roommate who were under varying degrees of June's spell. She ruled us like a harem, telling us what to do, when to do it, whether or not to go to class etc. I think I must have been her favorite because while I roomed with Genius, I slept five out of six nights with June. She would hold me in her arms until I fell asleep and I'd shake so badly the bed would tremble. We never went beyond cuddling. It never occurred to me there could be more. June must have known however.

She was very catholic and dragged me to 6 o'clock mass frequently. Every now and then she would come back from Mass and say that we couldn't sleep together anymore because she had confessed and the priest said that we shouldn't. I told her I couldn't see how it could possibly be a sin because we were just expressing our love for each other. That is the way my first year went. June kept me away from class enough doing chores for her that I managed to flunk out and lose my scholarship.

Over Christmas vacation, I returned to Franklin, I was hanging around with my high school gang when Colleen asked me to double date with her on New Year's Eve. Her new boyfriend wanted her to find a friend for his friend. I said, "Sure, why not?"

We all went out on New Year's Eve. The guys weren't from the area and wanted to know where we could find a bar to go and drink, even though all of us were under 21. Drinking wasn't a big deal for me since my parents allowed me to drink some even as a child. My parents weren't big drinkers but every Christmas and Thanksgiving my mother's family always served Tom Collins. As I recall, it is Seven-up with gin and a cherry.

They gave me and my cousin Joann a drink too (probably without alcohol in the beginning). But, as we got older they added a little alcohol and by the time I was 16, I was the bartender and mixing the drinks for everyone. Through high school there was always alcohol around at sleep overs and house parties. At Indiana University, the few dates I had we'd end up going to a certain bar we knew would serve any one.

Back to our New Year 's Eve dates, I told them about the bar and said that it was too bad the Starlight Club was sixty miles away. They weren't worried and said, no big deal. Gasoline was twenty-nine cents a gallon. And we were off. When we arrived at the Starlight Club, the weather was cold, but not freezing and the club was packed. We got in and even managed to get a booth. Party-goers stood, sat on stools, some danced the cigarette smoke was thick, and the live band/jukebox played.

I started to order my usual drink, a Seven and Seven—a Seven-up with Seven Crown. I didn't like it much but I thought it sounded sophisticated.

The waitress said "hey, we have a deal, anyone that can drink three Zombies and walk away, gets their money back".

"Well hell, "I thought "I can handle three drinks". Colleen agreed and so she and I ordered Zombies. Fortunately, the guys didn't order them. The Zombie was a good drink –three or four types of rum, pineapple, and orange fruit juice. The drink went down so easy and seemed like it was actually healthy with that fruit juice. When we finished the third one, I didn't feel so well and asked if we could go. The guys said sure. As I walked out of the bar, I felt faint and grabbed onto a man in a gray suit.

I had consumed all kinds of alcohol and thought I could handle about anything. One farmer in the area sold moonshine to the teenagers, which he kept secured in the pumpkins on his front porch. The ritual was you'd hand him a dollar and he'd hand you a half-pint of moonshine. You would then stand in the headlights of the running car and down the whole bottle without stopping to take a breath. If you took more than a drag off a cigarette as a chaser, you were considered a wimp. During our Halloween excursions in high school we went around turning over outhouses and kicking over ash cans we used to buy a pint of orange-flavored gin, which we would use to spike our Pepsi's while we drove around causing trouble. I had participated in these shenanigans for years, often as the driver with no problem.

But those three Zombies had me getting out of the car every five miles being sick on our way back to Franklin. This was during my Catholic stage and I knew New Year 's Day is a holy day of obligation. We were all staying at Judy's house and I knew the next day Ruth Ann would drag me out of bed to go to mass. People must have thought I was very devoted because I spent the entire service knelt on the kneeling bench. I was praying alright—praying I'd live through the day and that I wouldn't be sick during the service. It cured me. I've only been drunk 2 other times in my life and both were because of a mistake made with what I was drinking.When school was out, June came to my house and told my mother that she was transferring to Ball State Teachers College and that I should go with her. I would have signed up for boot camp in hell if June asked me to.

I think my mother was happy to send me off, so away I went after taking June with me to summer camp. I had agreed to work this year since I had lost my scholarship. I went to Muncie, Indiana to look for a room and a job. I had spent the morning looking around and went to a drugstore for lunch. Following my usual pattern, I made friends with the waitresses and was chatting about what I was doing.

She said "Wait here a minute, I have someone who wants to talk to you".

It turned out to be the drugstore owner and he told me that his family had a pool and wanted to rent the pool house – which had a kitchen and a bathroom for $25 per month. He also offered me a job. I was overjoyed and called June right away. But she told me she had already found a place that was free because she would babysit the owner's kid. I was brokenhearted and knew that I would have to get a roommate as I couldn't afford the rent alone.

I went back to the housing center and found a seemingly nice young woman who was looking for a place. So it was settled. After I moved in, things went okay at first, Irene, my roommate, though academically smart turned out to be not the brightest bulb. She tried to cook beans and seasoned them with pork rind snacks, and bought raw noodles to munch on. Her older sister, a school teacher, who was there more often than not.

They buttered up the landlord and landlady and Irene flirted with their 19-year-old son. Soon the landlords were taking Irene places with them and treating me coldly. They gave Irene a part-time job and before long found they didn't need me anymore. I took a job at the local theatre as a cashier. I took a cab home at 11 and got the same cab driver.

Von Lamb, otherwise known as Lamby-pie. It soon became a habit for us to go out to eat after I got off work. I dated him off and on for about a year. He was a perfect gentleman, never made anything even resembling a pass. Kind of makes you wonder. But I was delighted. Von was a mechanic in the daytime and before long turned me on to a car that had been left in his shop that I could buy for $100. It was a battered '38 Ford (this was 1951).It had mechanical brakes and a manifold heater. Which Von told me could easily be converted to hydraulic brakes and a regular heater if I was willing to do the work myself. I told him I had no experience as a mechanic and he reassured me not to worry and that he would guide me step by step. And he did exactly that.

While I worked on my car, he worked on the car next to me while telling me where each bolt and screw needed to go. That car was a godsend since the temperature that winter got to 22 degrees below, and I lived about 3 miles from campus. I even drove it back and forth to Franklin on several occasions with no problem. It was the color of wine and I painted the beat up bumpers with silver paint (Kentucky chrome). I added fresh tar on the soft roof to keep it from leaking. That car lasted until three days before I went into the Marine Corps when it threw a rod. I suspect it may have been committing suicide.

Milestone 14

When I transferred to Ball State, I no longer was able to pursue recreation. Instead, I decided to try a speech and drama major. I had always loved theatre and performed in many high school plays. By age twelve, flush with babysitting money, I used to sneak away from Franklin, take a bus to Indianapolis and go to the Old English Theatre. While my mother thought I was watching Roy Rogers, I was actually watching Hamlet, Kiss And Tell, Tobacco Road, etc. I even saw Dame Judith Anderson in Medea. I coveted that role and the role of "the hare-lipped girl" in Tobacco Road. I never got a chance at either role, but was sure I would have been magnificent in them.

I performed in "Taming of the Shrew" and "Outward Bound," and my favorite role – one of the weird sisters in "The Play That Shall Not Be Named." When the opportunity arose to help a coach get his PhD in swimming in order to teach at the college pool and lifeguard, I quit my job at the movie theatre. Another student who helped the coach was a beautiful men.

He was probably about 5'8" but his shoulder width and "wingspan" were incredible. He was very dark and every muscle in his body was perfectly outlined. His hair was dark brown and seemed to circle his head like a cap. I usually stood slightly behind him so I could admire the ripple of the muscles in his back and legs.

We were in a folk dancing class together and, for extra credit, the class held an open dance every Wednesday night. He invited me to go with him early in the semester and it became a ritual. We would dance, go out for a drink and then he'd drop me home—nothing more. No idea how I kept finding these guys— Gaydar? I never figured out whether I was lucky, unapproachable, or totally undesirable—however the undesirable part didn't work with everyone. Some of the guys I dated (generally only once) seemed to find me plenty desirable, but wrestling matches in the front seats of cars, never turned me on.

One of the perks the coach promised us was the opportunity to be a lifeguard at the city pool in the summer. Most of the students were going home, so I got the job and an opportunity to hire someone else. Obviously, I wanted June and so I took her and my instructor's badge to the lake and taught her lifesaving in one day. Biggest mistake of my life! – More on that later.

Muncie Indiana is nicknamed "little Chicago." It was a summertime hangout for some of the Chicago gangsters who came to cool off. One gangster in particular, known as "The Squirrel." We often saw him gliding around in his fancy car with reinforced doors and bullet proof windows. Maybe because of this influence, many of our local teens were downright dangerous. They often came to the local pool to horse around and they got generally rowdy. One kid in particular liked to do a fancy spin off the slide which shot him into deep water and was absolutely against the rules. I warned him twice and then told him to get out.

He came up to me laughing and said "You really think you can put me out?" He was not tall, but well-muscled with light skin and almost white hair.

I said, "Yes. You have to leave if I have to get down from this chair and take you myself".

He laughed again and said "You wouldn't dare."

Wrong thing to say. I jumped down in front of him. He was about 16 and for a minute, looked about 12. He said, "Are you seriously going to try?!"

"Yes.", I replied.

He re-considered; then said "You don't know who you are talking to, but I like your guts. I'm going to do you a favor and leave"

And, he did.

After he left, he came to the fence and said, "What happens when I come tomorrow?"

I said "We start fresh, so it depends on you."

He said "You will never have no more problems."

And I never did. The other kids started to respect me (or fear Donny... I never knew which). He walked me to the car at night. Once, he even carried an injured child to my car and another time he went with me to the emergency room. Accidents were common at the pool and I accompanied others to the emergency a lot. The male lifeguards always felt that since I was a woman and "motherly" I should be the one to take them in.

Once I brought in a bleeding child and handed him off to the ER staff. Then fainted. After that, it became protocol for the head nurse to tell the others where to put the child and for them to automatically give me a container of smelling salts. I was fine with emergencies up to the point that it was out of my hands, but once the nurses took over, down I'd go.

Donny was always looking out for me, and even walked me home once when my car wouldn't start. The one time he didn't protect me sticks out in my mind. It was a blazing hot summer day and with the humidity in Indiana, everyone was dripping sweat. The pool was jammed. A skinny red-faced guy was staggering along the walk toward the deep end. His face was flaming red and he had obviously been sipping the grape too much.

As he drew level with my chair, I said, "Hey buddy, go back and get a shower. You are obviously too overheated and the shock could kill you".

He muttered the usual two-word suggestion and dove right in. I had anticipated that and had already thrown off my hat, sunglasses, whistle, and dropped the towel I covered myself with. I hit the water about 30 seconds after he went in. I dove to the bottom and there he sat, almost yoga style. I could easily have done the chin lift and cross chest carry but being annoyed I used another technique. I slid my fingers from the back of his head to the front and grabbed a handful of hair. Luckily his hair was long enough that I got a good grip, kicked off the bottom and headed for the top. I shoved him against the ladder and directed, "up!" and up he went. He staggered to the fence, threw up a bunch of water, and staggered to the gate without a backward look.

As I gathered my things I glared at Donny who was doubled over with laughter. He managed to say (while giggling) "I knowed youze could haul his ass up."

Soon, I too was laughing. In my time as a lifeguard, I pulled out a total of 22 people. Only one, a little girl of 12 who had been trying to carry her sister in deep water, thanked me. I have probably taught about one thousand people to swim, and I suppose that counts for something too. June accused me of "robbing the cradle", saying Donny was my boyfriend, but she was busy making eyes at a tall dark-haired young man named Tom. He came often to the pool and started taking her home, which sometimes took two or three hours. June had talked me into becoming a Catholic and I was in the process of being confirmed.

The young roly-poly priest asked me to stay after class once so he could talk to me. He started telling me it was not a good idea to date "town boys" and that I should stick to college students. He said the local boys might be married and not tell me. It didn't make sense until I realized that I was not the only female lifeguard at the city pool. I told him my roommate was also a lifeguard and had been dating a local guy named Tom. He told me Tom was married and had a 2 year old daughter and a 4 month old son. When I told June this, she said she didn't care and that he wanted to leave his wife but was having trouble because they were Catholic.

By this time June and I were sharing a room and I was furious, upset, and wildly jealous. At about that same time, another student in our housing gave me the book "The Well of Loneliness" by Radclyffe Hall, a lesbian novel published in 1928 that became "the bible" of all lesbians at that time. I am amazed at the number of young lesbian women today who have not read it. It is equivalent to never having seen or not recognizing "Fried Green Tomatoes" for the lesbian cult movie that it is.

That same student had seen the interaction between June and I and had figured out what was going on long before I did. I stuck around till January, very unhappy. Finally, totally disgusted, I headed to Franklin on a Friday. The highway happened to take me past the post office where I spotted a picture of a woman in service standing under a palm tree. I immediately parked and headed upstairs. I had known a woman who had been in the coast guard. She had taught swimming to new coast guard recruits while stationed in Florida. She stayed and taught out of a hotel.

I knew I could do that and when I got out I could go to college and not work. I dashed up to the coast guard office, only to be faced with the sign on the door which read "we are out to lunch" I turned to go have lunch while I waited, and was met by a woman marine stepping out of her office.

"They are out to lunch dear. Would you like to wait in here? Would you like a Coca-Cola?" she offered.

Who could pass that up? My god she was good. It took her less than an hour to turn me around and swear me in. I was off to the Marine Corp. June ultimately married Tom and they went on to have three little boys. After that, she dumped him and married again. The last time I saw her was a few years after her second marriage when we were both at a teacher's convention in Indianapolis.

After an interesting afternoon we went back to her hotel. She stripped to her undies, lay on the bed and invited me to join her—just like old times. Then she turned to me and said "promise not to rape me." Insulted and angry, I blew up and told her how I felt all those years ago. I then turned and stormed out, but not before saying, "if you want me, you know where to find me." That was the last I ever heard from her.

Milestone 15

On a Sunday, approximately a week before my birthday I found myself on a sleeper car headed for Washington DC. The final destination was Beaufort, South Carolina and eventually Paris Island Marine Corps Base. The next morning, prior to arriving in Washington DC, I found myself seated across from a very attractive lady. I was wearing an "Eisenhower" jacket, which was all the rage at the time. She commented on my jacket and then said she "shouldn't do this," and then started opening a large box beside her. She handed me a white pen with red and blue letters that said "I like Ike."

She said she was delivering them to Republican headquarters and she was giving me the first one. I was turning 21 shortly and going to have the right to vote for the first time. My parents were dyed in the wool Republican conservatives from the Midwest, and I knew no better. It was the first (and last) time that I ever voted Republican, but who knew? While in Washington, on her recommendation, I had an order of cherrystone clams. I'd never had them before and loved them them.

After boarding the train for Beaufort, I got an idea of what the next few months would be like. There were a number of women recruits on the same car with me, and we went to the dining car together. In those days, dining on a train was a gourmet experience complete with full (and fancy) place settings. Each place setting included a finger bowl with a couple of slices of lemon beside it.

Finger bowls were used to wash ones fingers during the meal. Before I could say anything the young woman beside me sipped from her finger bowl, squeezed some lemon into it and took another sip. As I stared at her in amazement she said, "That is really not fit to eat." Automatically my "smart-ass-ery" came out and I said, "I'll show them what I think of it", and dipped my fingers in and wiped them on a napkin.

I was later to discover that I had stumbled into the last platoon to recruit female non-high-school graduates. We were known affectionately as "the goon platoon" and were twice as large as the average platoon. However, by graduation our numbers were reduced by 25% including in their number the little finger bowl sipper.

There were a number of interesting characters in my platoon that I recall affectionately, even today. Most of them were 18 and I became a kind of mother or big sister to the group. When I first got there, there were 5 Hawaiians and one little blonde girl named Posey. Later they were joined by "Tennessee A." Tennessee became my friend and we stayed friends for years. Later she became a bartender in a gay bar in San Francisco. Her "gaydar" must have been going crazy because she gave me the book "Women's Barracks" to read.

Curiously enough, that book is still featured on the "gay bookshelf" in Barnes and Noble along with "Spring Fire" and "Pound of Salt." I haven't checked the copyrights but those books have got to be at least 60 years old.

One of my favorites was a cute little blonde, "Jonie W." She was very immature and homesick. I tucked her in every night and kissed her on the forehead and never thought anything about it. On one occasion too many she giggled in line and lost us our cigarette break. That evening a stomp-y dyke named Bobbie and a group of her cohorts came after her. They were going to give her a "GI shower" - a cold shower with a steel brush and sand soap, one of the favored forms of punishment in boot camp.

She ran and hid behind me. Bobby came up to me and said "get out of the way". I said "sorry guys, but you've got to go through me". I don't know what I was thinking – Bobbie was 5 inches taller, a workout freak, and mean-looking as hell.

We stared at each other for a few minutes and then she (Bobbie) said "well, damn, keep her in line!" and they all walked away.

I think I had to to change my drawers. From that time on, Jonie clung to me like an abalone on its favorite rock. Still don't know why Bobbie walked away. I've done that a few times in my life. The aggressors always give in and afterwards, I wonder why. Somehow I must project a much stronger persona than I really am.

Milestone 16

The most important event that took place in boot camp occurred one night when I was standing watch duty. We all had an opportunity to stand a two-hour watch, during which we drank cokes and smoked cigarettes to our heart's content. I always took at least one watch and sometimes two in a row. There was very little we were required to do, unless one of the girls became sick and we had to call for help. I read, wrote letters, and just overall enjoyed the privacy and quiet. At the end of each shift before waking our relief, we checked the barracks to make sure everything was fine. One night in May, I made the pass through the barracks and found two empty bunks. I couldn't understand where the occupants could be; I checked the bathroom, dayroom and the laundry room.

I didn't think they would have gone outside as male marines with rifles patrolled the barracks. The only other space was a huge gear closet where the mops, sanders, polishers, etc. were kept. I didn't expect to find anybody but opened the door and Oh. My. God. There they three girls were on the floor, sans pajamas, wrapped up in some lover's knot I had never seen before. I can still see it. It's burned into my brain and I still cannot figure out how they managed it. I was struck almost dumb, but squeezed out a tinny "excuse me", closed the door and quietly went back to my office.

I didn't wake my relief, but instead drank two more Cokes (wishing it was Jim Beam instead) and chain-smoked cigarettes realizing that that was who I was—I'm a queer! But it did look like fun. When I finally had the courage to check the barracks again, all the bunks were filled and I couldn't (for the life of me) even remember which ones had been empty. I am ashamed to say that it took me 67 years to figure out who one of the women was, although I had a perfect clue. The night before we left for our new duty stations, a cute little blonde chick came around to my bunk and slipped into the sack with me. She stuck her head under the covers so no one would see her and asked where I was going to be stationed. I said "the supply school at Camp Lejeune".

She said that was too bad because she was going to the marine airbase at Cherry Point. We snuggled for a while and then she went back to her bunk. That is the last I ever saw of her. She must have been one of the "gear closet girls" to be brave enough to crawl in bed with me. They must have sweated bullets thinking they would be exposed and court-martialed after I had opened the door. When I didn't expose them I guess they realized I was one of them and that gave her courage to jump in bed with me.

Another notable event during boot camp included a trip to Beaufort to Mickey's Shoe Store to buy shoes. I don't know why, since we were all issued high top boots (which killed us). Mickey's shoes were oxfords that we had to take back to the barracks and dye cordovan brown to match the uniforms. They were not Government Issue but we were given no choice, our corporal took us there and ordered us to buy them. Mickey, the owner was selling at least 20 pairs every 2 weeks. I think he must have been ready to move to the Riviera.

Milestone 17

Another event occurred on April 14. The Marine Corp had "interesting" rules for us, which may have changed. I certainly hope they have. When I was there, winter uniforms for women Marines included scarves, gloves, cotton stockings and a girdle. On April 15th Marines start wearing summer uniforms. The weather has nothing to do with it... except in San Francisco, where one wears winter uniforms year round. This particular April 14 a new general was introduced to the troops with a parade around the mile long field. That particular day, the temperature was 105F on Perris Island. Women Marines were chosen to lead the parade. The commanding officer of the women's corp was a tiny lieutenant from Alabama. With a loud mouth and a southern accent.

She said, "Ladies if any of you feel you are going to faint, be sure you die, because if you embarrass me in front of those fine officers, I will personally kill you".

You will remember I mentioned girdles? And If you don't know what a sand flea is, you are much better off. Paris Island has lots of them. The girdle required was the "living girdle" with tiny air holes all over it. I don't know how they managed it but a sand flea found every hole in every girdle and bit and bit the respective wearer. They also swarmed our eyes, nose, and mouth - any place there was moisture. The only saving grace was that women marines did not carry rifles.

As we passed the review stand, instead of presenting rifles, we saluted. And instead of "throwing the salute away" as instructed, we drew our hands over our faces to release the sand fleas. If this wasn't bad enough, a number of male marines fainted as they went around and as a result, we had to do it again. Our lieutenant was so proud of us - as none of the women even stumbled. As a reward, she ordered huge steaks and chocolate syrup to go with the ice-cream at the mess hall. At graduation in June, I was given two weeks to go home as the class at Camp Lejeune did not start until later. My mother paraded me all over town in my uniform (like a new puppy). The gang I hung out with wanted to know if the women marines were full of queers. I told them that I hadn't noticed.

I realized why I had never really bonded with that group. I always felt different and naturally, I was. I never really missed any of them although, I would have liked to have seen Ruby Jo and Luella from Columbus. On overnights they used to like to play make-out games as in "does Billy kiss you like this?" I could have introduced some innovations to their games. At Camp Lejeune I became involved with an 18 year old named Gwen, from Ithaca New York. I'd like to tell you how it started, but I haven't the slightest idea. I remember once sitting with Bobbie on the back stoop of the barracks, I told her that my life had totally changed and I didn't quite know how to handle it, even when I saw it coming straight toward me (as Gwen came down the path). Gwen and I were making out in sneaky places, like the edge of the swamp—but not the gear closet. I was scared of that. We even got weekend passes and went to Cape Fear, North Carolina to a hotel.

Outside of eating horseshoe crab on a riverboat restaurant, we spent most of our time in bed. Neither one of us knew what we were doing, we mainly just fumbled around. It wasn't very satisfactory but was exciting as hell. At the same time, I was dating an Italian guy named Al, who had been a med student until the Marine Corps (in their infinite wisdom) transferred him to the chemical warfare section in the south, somewhere. At the same time, there was this exotic-looking woman named Kathy (in my barracks) who was always watching me. I ran into her once in boot camp.

She was a platoon ahead of me. She was on watch one weekend day when we were playing soccer out back, I was running one way and looking the other. Not a good idea. I ran into an 18" high concrete pole intended to keep cars from parking. I flew over the top and knocked myself unconscious. I'm told four or five of the players carried me into the barracks and put a cloth on my head. Cathy sat with me and kept me talking so I wouldn't fall asleep. I learned she was half Native American and half Irish. She had thick curly dark brown hair and gold eyes.

The other interaction I had with Cathy in boot camp occurred one morning when we were falling out for the chow line. She stopped me and said "Earrings Private." That scared the socks off me because wearing earrings with one's uniform was definitely a court-marshal offense. Similarly, appearing in uniform without Revlon "Independence Red" lipstick was also a court martial offense. I doubt seriously it would have happened in either case; however I did hear of recruits being chewed out and given extra duty if they appeared without lipstick or with a lipstick shade that didn't match the red cord on our caps.

One of the things I noticed was that at the end of the month, Cathy always had money for Cokes when the rest of us were broke. One afternoon I asked her how that happened and she said that she knew how to manage money. I asked her if she would manage mine and she said "sure". After that, I was never broke at the end of the month again. Over time, Cathy began to spend more and more time with me as Gwen spent less and less. Finally, Gwen seemed to disappear out of my life altogether. As in the beginning I have little memory of the end, but she will always be the first woman I went to bed with.

I still have very tender feelings for her. Cathy took up where Gwen left off, making out with me behind the sand dunes and on the edge of the swamp. One afternoon I decided I wanted a Coke, but the Coke machine was empty. Our barracks were next to a building that housed two bars. The one downstairs was for men only and opened at 5. The one upstairs was for women and their male companions. It opened at 7 and served only beer and milkshakes.

The building that had the two bars was lovingly called "the slop chute". That particular afternoon I was really thirsty and went to the downstairs bar. Lots of guys were standing around outside so I asked a little Puerto Rican guy to get me a Coke. He said; "No problema Chiquita" he brought me a big coke in a glass and started to engage me in conversation. I started back to the barracks and he said, "No, No, you must talk to me."

He kept begging me to stay but I went back to my barracks. By the time I had drunk half the Coke, my throat began to sting. I took a couple more sips and told Cathy that there was something wrong with my drink. It wasn't long before I started itching in some very sensitive spots. I told Cathy and she started cracking up and said "Oh My God, Spanish fly; it's supposed to be an aphrodisiac."

"What do I do?" I wailed, and she said "not much." She managed to con our corporal out of some codeine, gave that to me and put me in a cold shower. After a while it finally let up. If I could have identified that little jerk in the crowd of Marines I would have performed "Castratus Completus" with a dull knife! Frequently Cathy and I would go to the "slop chute" in the evening for a beer and a milkshake. I was the milkshake drinker, but people kept pouring beer in it and so I finally gave up.

Milestone 18

In the women's bar a juke box, small dance floor with tables scattered around the outside of it made up its decor. One evening a very tall, handsome Marine sitting at the table across the dance floor, got up and came over to our table and asked me to dance. I have never been a good dancer and it felt very awkward, but he was gorgeous. His thick thick curly blonde hair, brilliant blue eyes, great dimples, and a cleft chin with a brilliant, white smile that nearly knocked me off my chair.

I learned later he was called "Ski with the beautiful teeth." He danced me through three songs and I said "Hey your girlfriend sitting over there," I looked around his shoulder and behind us, "is going to get annoyed."

He said, "I am from Bingington, NY, and she is too. Mom told me to be nice to her, but she is just a friend, she's not my date".

Cathy didn't seem to mind, so when he asked me for a date the next evening, I said "sure".

Actually when he came to pick me up the next evening, the girl came out of her squad room at the other end of the building. He said that he had totally forgotten asking her. It may not have been a date to him, but it definitely had been to her. It turned out he was a regular around the military and "played the field." Quite a few of the women had big crushes on him and they were very envious of me. Apparently he had never gone out with one woman more than once or twice, but we were together almost every day.

Before long, he started picking me up and carrying me into the middle of the swamp to a dry, sandy knoll he knew about. It was there that I had my first heterosexual, sexual experience. It didn't do much for me, but he was sweet and kind and I wanted to please him. The bad part was when I came home and took a shower, Cathy had to pick the ticks off my butt. My mother had always given me the idea that sex was a duty and that only men liked it.

Consequently, I thought this was all normal. He talked of marriage and children. He wanted 11 boys and 2 girls – "a football team with cheerleaders," he'd said.

One night I told him that since I'd be graduating soon at the top of my class in supply school, I was choosing San Francisco as my duty station. Cathy had talked me into it, saying I would love it out there. I didn't know why at the time. I thought he'd be upset, but actually he wasn't. He said that he was being transferred too – to Camp Pendleton. He was a staff sergeant and wanted to go up the ranks to become an officer. To do that, he had to have overseas duty. At Camp Lejeune he was a football player and since he had volunteered to go to Korea, he needed a three-week refresher course at Camp Pendleton. When he came back he would be able to choose any duty station that he wanted. As it happened, it didn't work that way.

He was captured in Korea within a month. He was returned in the prisoner exchange but came straight to Oak Knoll Naval Hospital. I went to see him immediately, even though I had committed to Cathy by that time. I could only see him through glass. I could not go near him. I was glad we'd exchanged smiles, stares, whatever. Three weeks later he died from virulent Tuberculosis. Damn war. He was the sweetest, kindest guy. He'd left a week before my transfer and I spent the next week entirely with Cathy. On the fourth of July, Cathy and I went to Onslow Beach, part of Camp Lejeune. They had a dressing room and a snack bar where one could buy beer and hot dogs. We had fun bodysurfing and splashing each other and walking with great care because the little Puerto Rican Marines were fond of sticking their cigarettes in the sand, fire side up.

In late afternoon, we wandered down among the sand dunes where we were totally out of sight and decided to make out. In the middle of a mad smooth, a guy came running around the next dune and said "Hey let me play too". We leapt up at the speed of light, forgetting cigarette dangers or anything else. We dove into the dressing room, threw on our clothes, jumped on the camp bus and rode back to the barracks.

When we got back to our barracks we were shaking in our boots. If one were discovered engaging in gay behavior, they ripped any chevrons off your sleeve, took back the Marine Corps emblems, marched you to the gate, threw you out with all your belongings, handing you a discharge stamped "undesirable". That could have a serious effect on one's ability to get work afterwards. I definitely didn't want that and managed to avoid it in my service career.

Another interesting event happened on a hot summer's day after that when someone told me to open the door first thing in the morning. Because we had air-conditioning it was pleasantly cool in the squad bay but blazing hot outside. As I opened the door, 3-4 inch-lines of roaches and other insects rolled into the squad bay. They had been jammed up against the base of the door. Out of the center came a big, black furry spider. Its head and body together were at least 5" long. Never having been a fan of arachnids, I screamed and ran down the center aisle to where Sargent Ring was calling "0530 – hit the deck".

Without hesitation I leaped into her arms screaming: "Kill it! Kill it! Kill it!"... She said "Well somebody better kill it, cuz I ain't carrying this around all day". At which point she dropped me on my butt.

This scenario is probably the forerunner of what happened next. Sargent Ring was a rather short, stocky, and unattractive woman, somewhere in her 30s. She was in charge of the squad bay and all activities within it such as changing sheets, doing laundry and assigning chores. I don't think she had ever noticed me before, but shortly after the spider event, she invited me into her little nook. We chatted for a few minutes and then she made a very inappropriate suggestion letting me know that she could close the door so that we would not be bothered.

I said, "no thank you; I'm Cathy's girl and I do not cheat". I was using Cathy as an excuse with Sgt. Ring, as I still was questioning my orientation at this point.

She reminded me she was in charge of duty assignment and asked how I felt about the laundry room. I told her "That would be fine, thank you very much" and walked out.

The laundry room was everyone's "nightmare" assignment. It consisted of three washing machines and three strange dryers that were built into the wall with a rack that slid out to hold clothes. There was no way of closing the dryers completely and the heat poured out of them morning till night. The poor sap assigned this duty was to clean the washers inside and out, wipe down the dryer racks and scrub the floor on hands and knees. I did a good job and didn't make a peep of protest, though Cathy was pissed.

The temperatures outside were 104F and felt cool after stepping out of that laundry room. The next week, Sgt. Ring wiggled her eyebrows at me and looked at her nook. I smiled and nodded to the laundry room. So it went for five weeks. It never occurred to me to complain to the lieutenant or anyone else. I was very proud of myself and to tell the truth, I think Sgt. Ring would have been disappointed in me had I given in towards the end.

It had become a game, and I won. At the end of 5 weeks Sgt. Ring and Cpl. Kitts went AWOL to Pennsylvania. I have no idea why. The job was taken over by Cpl. Joy who introduced herself as "the joy boy from Rogers O, hello, hello, hello!"

Suddenly, it was like living in a musical comedy. She sang and danced everything, even orders. When she looked at the orders and saw what was happening to me, she was horrified and called me in to find out what was up. I of course refused to give up information about "family" and just said that we had a falling out.

She said "Yeah I bet, she suggested things you refused?"

I smiled. I never had bad feelings towards Sgt. Ring. I guess because I knew I'd won. For the next few weeks, Cathy and I hid beer in milkshake cups and sneaked it into Ring and Kitts (they were under house arrest). I know it's weird, but I'd do the same thing all over again. I was given $350 to pay my way to San Francisco (by way of Indiana). However, even though Cathy and I were not committed to each other, I decided to save the money to bring her to San Francisco when she got discharged. I don't know why I was sure she would be discharged soon. I can't remember what she told me.

I went to the air force base outside Washington and hitched a ride on a national guard plane headed for Indianapolis. I was home for a couple weeks and then went to Chanute field AFB in Illinois, planning to hitch a ride to California. That was on a Thursday. I was due in San Francisco by midnight Saturday night. No planes were headed that way all day and I slept on the women's bathroom floor that night and Friday night. I was getting very nervous when finally a call went out for a plane going to Tinker Air Force Base. It was an old B-2 bomber with 2 pilots and no extra seats. They put a parachute on me and sat me on the Bomb-bay doors.

They said: "hold onto the rip cord handles and if the doors open automatically, count to ten before you pull it". The parachute was soft and I was very tired and fell asleep. I figured if they accidentally dropped me my hand would jerk the rip cord and so I slept all the way to Tinker AFB. I happened to get there just in time to catch a ride on a gooney bird headed to Santa Ana. There were about 20 male marines in the cargo bay and two female marines camped out in the tail section. More than half of them had coffee cans in front of them being sick. I had never been sick on a plane, and I don't think I would have been that time either, except for the odor from everyone else's vomit. The overpowering smell soon added me to the coffee can crew. I thought Santa Ana was right next to Los Angeles and was not worried about making it to San Francisco by midnight. I caught a rickety bus at the main gate which turned out to be full of Mexican farm workers and even a crate of chickens. It was light when I got on the bus but dark when I got to LAX and I was getting nervous.

I caught the first flight to San Francisco but it didn't put me in till 11:45. If I had only remembered what I had learned in boot camp, I would have turned myself into the first MPs I saw in the airport. I only had about 10 minutes to log in and I didn't know how far away the Marine Corp Depot of supplies at 100 Harrison Street was. I also thought that they wouldn't fuss about being a few minutes late—I was wrong.

There are no female barracks in San Francisco. Women Marines live in rooms or apartments—which is one of the reasons I chose that duty station. That way Cathy and I would be able to live together without being caught. You worked 8-4 on weekdays and twice a month attended a close-order drill and exercise period. The captain on duty was very nice, put me in a car and checked me into a hotel. He told me to report to the parking lot at 8 a.m. Monday morning.

Milestone 19

The next day, I went for lunch at the Marines' memorial coffee shop on Sutter Street in San Francisco. An attractive woman next to me started to chat, asking if I was new in town. We talked for quite a while and since I was new she offered to show me the city. She showed me the entire city (including her apartment and her bed). I spent the night both Saturday and Sunday. It was a revelation. I had never had that kind of experience with a woman before.

Anything before was just inexperienced fumbling. She was older, experienced, and talented—very talented. She took me to dinner at a gay restaurant on Polk Street and a drag show on Broadway. To really understand that, gay people did not, as a rule, give their last name, where they worked and where they lived.

Just taking me to her apartment was a big concession on her part because there was always the chance of blackmail. Early Monday morning she said, "let me take you to your hotel, because I have to get to work."

About 7 a.m. she dropped me off in front of my hotel. I raced upstairs, was dressed and on a cable car in 15 minutes. I jumped on a streetcar to Key terminal, hoofed over to 100 Harrison with 5 minutes to spare. There were two other new arrivals and so they stood us at the head of the line when we fell in. Our commanding officer Lt. S.L. walked out.

I prayed the tarmac would open up and swallow me. I think she was praying the same thing.

The Lieutenant almost stumbled, coughed and turned back fully in control to put us through our paces. It was my weekend tour guide. As we were dismissed, she asked me to come to her office, as there was a paper I needed to sign. When I got there, standing at attention, she said "As you were," and then continued: "How good is your memory private?"

I told her. "Unfortunately, I have a terrible memory." I told her I could not even remember what I had done this weekend.

She said , "I hope that is true because unfortunately I have to follow the rules. Because you were late, I will have to take away your private first class stripe and bust you down to private for a couple of months."

The only effect that had was to lose me about $15 a month from my salary. I think she was afraid I would make a stink, but I told her I understood completely, I deserved it, and was grateful to her for everything. She said that this is one of the few times that she regretted being in service.

"Dismissed private."

Milestone 20

I was assigned to the colonel's office to handle the filing which was set up on the Navy's filing system. The Navy filing system is not alphabetical. They had basically touched on it during supply school, saying that it took months to learn and they hoped that we would never come in contact with it. I was trained by a pregnant civilian woman who was going on maternity leave. The training lasted 2 weeks, at the end of which, I knew nothing. Each type of equipment, ammunition or supply had its own unique series of numbers. For example Road clearing equipment started with the numbers 105 and ended with five different numbers for each different piece.

I lasted about two weeks, at which point the colonel very politely transferred me to the next office which was in charge of acquiring road building equipment. I shared the office with two "fairy hawks" who liked to brag on Mondays about the number of queers they had beaten up over the weekend. One Monday morning they limped in, bruised, battered, and cut up. They told me that they had picked up a tall skinny blonde kid on Saturday and talked him into going into the alley with them.

As soon as he realized what they were there for he said "There is only one thing l like better than sex, and that is fighting." Then he set about punching, kicking, and hammering the crap out of both of them. One of them said, "he did some of that crazy Asian shit. There ought to be a law against it." I said mildly, "Poor guys," and I went to get a cup of tea.

On the way back I managed to "accidentally" trip over one guy's sore foot and pour a hot cup of tea on the other one. I was, "so sorry." Bastards. As far as the rest of my job was concerned I think I mainly endeared myself to the North Koreans. I certainly didn't endear myself to the managers of the companies that were building the machines. Even though they were painted with camouflage, the road graders and snow plows were very large.

It is almost impossible to sneak a road grader up Hamburger Hill. Every time one got blown up they would be demanding another one and I would be on the phone trying to arrange it. The guys at the companies got very tired of the sound of my voice. I tried not to think about the guys driving the machines and hoped they were able to dive off before the equipment was blown up. I thought at the time that we should have brought all our resources to bear and won that war. Today I am even more certain.

Milestone 21

Aside from being on-duty, living in San Francisco was like a whole different world. The first weekend, my tour guide showed me a side of life I had never imagined. The following weekend, I got a funny phone call from someone very flirty who invited me out for a drink. I knew that it had to be someone who knew me because she got through to my room in the hotel. I agreed and an hour later, I met my ole buddy "Tennessee" – the recruit from boot camp who had the bunk next to mine and had loaned me the book "Women's Barracks." I hadn't seen her in years. She asked if I wanted to go to "Mona's Candlelight" (a gay bar on Broadway), and I said sure. She said that she wondered in boot camp how long it would take for me to find out who I really was."

She said that she watched me tuck those three cuties in every night and that she knew that I had walked in on a couple of her friends. I told her that a couple of women in North Carolina had clued me in and we both laughed. Tennessee stayed in San Francisco when she got out and became a bartender at a local gay bar. As far as I know, she is still there. We got so that we hung out at Mona's. On about the third night, an interesting looking person walked in the bar. I asked Tennessee, "Boy or girl?" She said, "Total butch". The woman had short black hair and was wearing a yachting cap, and men's shirt, and jeans. She circled the room, giving hugs and kisses to her friends and then made her way back to the bar.

She came straight to me and said, "You are new, you haven't had the pleasure of my acquaintance yet. My name is Billy Jack and I'm from Wichita Falls, Texas, What about you?" She hopped onto the barstool beside me and said, "Just for that, I will let you buy me a Coke."

I said, how come a Coke?"

And she said, "Because I like to be in charge at all times."

She later told me that she was under cover for the FBI and was always on duty. She was supposed to be searching for communists who were trying to recruit in the gay community but was so deep under cover that she couldn't even receive a paycheck or someone would rat her out. Therefore (she reasoned), it was up to the rest of us to help her survive.

Heh. I believe that like I believe the Brooklyn Bridge is for sale. I don't know quite how it happened, but before long, she had moved in with me at the hotel. One day, she even showed up for a meal in my uniform. That scared the crap out of me, so I went along with moving with her to another small apartment on Bush Street. It was full of lesbian couples, including the beautiful Ann D. the singer from Mona's Candlelight and "Crazy Sparrow" another boot camp friend who lived in the hotel first. I had ridden up in the elevator in the hotel, taking her to her room when she was drunk.

She took primal sexual behavior to a whole new level. I got her to her room and aimed her at her bed and ran the hell out, and locked my door. Ann D. was into kinky stuff and that had never been my cup of tea.

Billy called me one day and said, "Sparrow has gone wonky, better check her out."

When I arrived, Sparrow was wadding up and throwing money all over her room and threatening suicide. I gathered the money and tried to find out what was upsetting her. She kept repeating "It's filthy, it's filthy". Billy came to the door and I quietly told her to call the base and send and ambulance because Sparrow had really blown a fuse. I tried to give her back the money and asked her where it came from. It was more than $100. She said she got it from the owner of a Philippine restaurant in North Beach. I think the name was something like Be Yong See Kat. We all called it the "Boing Cat." She told me to keep the money. In retrospect, I suspect that she had had sex with the owner who was very friendly with all the lesbians. The Marine corpsmen came and took her to Oak Knoll Naval Hospital.

She was there until she got a discharge. It is not a bad place actually. I should know since I eventually ended up there myself—better to get a medical discharge than an undesirable one—but that will come later. Because I had to be up and at work at 8 a.m., I didn't go to the bars on weeknights, but Billy did. I was snuggly tucked in my Murphy bed about 11 o'clock when Billy came in with a guest on her arm. They didn't turn the light on, but I heard them whispering, first in the kitchen and then in the bathroom. The next thing I knew, a warm body slipped in bed next to me and the bed bounced as a third person crawled in. There was a bit more whispering and giggling. Then all fell silent and I went back to sleep.

I woke up in the morning with a warm body so close to me that she was breathing in my ear. When I turned to the right to see who was there, I nearly fainted.

I was staring into a pair of auburn eyes that matched the long auburn hair falling over her shoulders.

She was the sweetest, most beautiful girl I think I had ever seen. In a sexy husky voice, she said, "Hi, I am Jan."

I said, "Hi, I'm in love." She laughed. "I've got to get up and get to work," I said, sliding out of bed. She followed me. We went into the kitchen as Billy snored away and I made us tea and toast. She asked me where I worked and was surprised when I said that I was a Marine.

She said "I'm impressed."

And I said, "I'm enthralled. Will I see you later?" She said I would. She repeated her name and said it was Jan Evans, but actually it was Jean B and she was a long distance phone operator, from Fresno, and was only up for the weekend. She looked a lot like the actress Elaine Stewart.

When I got home that afternoon, she and Billie were already gone. I changed and made it to the bars in record time. I was told that Billy had a car and was looking for me. I stood out on the sidewalk, and sure enough, Billy and Jan rolled up in a big old sedan. We went to an Italian restaurant in North Beach and ate Pesto spaghetti (my new favorite), then went back to the bars.

Jan and I had two or three drinks, with Billy sticking to Coke - as usual. Then, out of the blue, "Crazy Sparrow" walked in. She was trying to start a fight, and generally making an ass of herself. Mona's was off-limits to her and she was so rowdy that Mother Frenchie threatened to call the MPs which would have gotten us all in a lot of trouble—me especially. Billy asked Sparrow why she was out of the hospital.

She said that she was on liberty, but needed to go back. So off we went to the car and loaded up. Billy drove, Jan next to her, then me, Sparrow, and the chick she had been making out with, in the back. Oak Knoll hospital is a good distance out Mac Arthur Blvd in the East Bay. Jan was a bit "tiddly" by this time and cuddled up to me and started nibbling on my ear. I had no idea what Billy would do under these circumstances so I played it very cool, but let her know that I liked it. We moved the next week to the house on Jackson Street and Jan was right there snuggling in the middle again. Billy slept in flannel pajamas, Jan slept in a black satin bra and black satin pajama bottoms. I was so in love, I hardly slept at all.

I didn't know quite what to do, I had sent Cathy plane money to come out and felt a certain amount of pressure to follow thru on that, but I was so in love with Jan, I was confused. One night, Jan and I managed to get Billy to go to the bars alone, but we stayed back and made love. Sex with Billy hade never meant much to me emotionally, but this time I was almost obsessed. It was just my luck that Cathy showed up two days after that. I wanted to scream, but I decided that the honorable thing was to go with Cathy. In retrospect, it was one of the worst decisions I've made in my life. Cathy happily moved in, Billy happily grabbed her stuff and Jan and moved to the third floor, and I was stuck for the next ten years. I've tried to find Jan several times over the years with no luck. The money Crazy Sparrow gave to me before she went to Oak Knoll was a godsend since Billy was stealing me blind, and in their wisdom the Marine Corps had classed me as a male marine and given me only $32 a month.

They were supposed to give me $130 more than that for room and board (this extra money was known as subs and quarters). I asked the guy handing me the money—can't you see that I am a woman? He said, sorry, I can only give you what it says here on the paper. So I went to see my lieutenant – the old tour guide. She said she would look into it, but I never heard another thing. As a result, I went to the Y and asked for a job as a swimming teacher. The room alone was $40 a month. They offered me the job of lifeguard on Saturday and Sunday for $10/hour for each afternoon. At last I was able to eat at least one meal a day. One day, when I came home, Billy announced that she had found us a cheaper room and had already started moving my things out there.

I had no idea why I went along with Billy, I really don't know what our relationship was. She lied and stole, but I fed her and let her stay with me. She was actually a fun companion and damn good in bed. She was the only experienced woman outside of my "tour guide" that I had yet encountered. I have always, since childhood, been able to tell when people were lying. My mother lied quite a bit—to my father, her friends and to me. Others did too, teachers, school friends, etc.

I had decided early on, that everyone lied to get approval or because they were afraid of something, so I never judged people for lying, I simply heard the truth behind their words and went on. My first committed girlfriend Cathy turned out to be the best liar I ever knew in my life. She once convinced a group of nuclear scientists that she was conversant with science involved in the Manhattan Project in Los Alamos. I had been reading tarot at a fancy party at the time and she discussed things with them for nearly an hour.

I later asked her how she managed. She laughed and said that they had told her lots of things that she probably shouldn't know. By lunchtime the next day, she had convinced a local chef that she had studied at Cordon Bleu. Cathy was one of the smartest women I have ever known. She never graduated from high school because she "froze" when faced with a test, but there was nothing that she couldn't discuss.

Milestone 22

The new room was in an old Victorian on Jackson St. three doors from Fillmore. It was at the end of the cable car line in 1952. We had 3 Chinese restaurants in close proximity, (the Green lantern and two others), two Chinese grocery stores (lovingly dubbed "the clean and the dirty" due to general tidiness). The waiter at the Green lantern would only allow the butches to order, he would never even look at a femme. The cashier at the dirty store was a girl between 8 and 12 who would always look us over to make sure we had nothing in our pockets. Across the street was the Foxes Den restaurant. That is where we got our daily meal. It consisted of one BLT sandwich and one carton of milk, which we split. We figured we were getting something from all four food groups and so we must be okay. When we had extra money we would gobble up Chinese food at the Green Lantern or go to a hot dog stand close to California St.

We were there often enough that we made friends with the woman that worked it. So much so, that when we showed up on Thanksgiving she piled our plates with dogs and all the trimmings and colas, for free. Her boyfriend, who was hanging with her, gave us each a shot of brandy. I can't say I liked it. But I downed it and smiled anyway. The other restaurant in the area was the Bon Vivant. It was a Jewish delicatessen run by a hippie couple as this the time the hippie movement had started. The husband was a beautiful tall young man with black hair down to his waist. The wife was a short chubby blonde who was always bustling and giggling. They had a tiny 3-year-old son who constantly wandered in the center of the U-shaped bar that enclosed the food.

When you came in, if he had gotten to know you, he would ask, "You like it thick or thin maybe?" He was so cute. We spent a great deal of time there as Cathy got called in for part-time work when they needed extra help. She often took her wages in food: lovely Matzo ball soup and Hungarian goulash.

I enshrined myself in their memory by making one of my more infamous faux pas. Written across the the bottom of every menu were the words "Everything avec smaltze". I said "Who is this Alec Smaltze guy? Is he the owner?"

Then Cathy (a transplanted New Yorker) and the whole family, including the little kid, busted out laughing. When Cathy was finally able to control herself, she explained to me that everything was cooked in chicken fat. I swear, they giggled at me for the next half hour. I didn't say much to them for the next week. I spoke mostly to a doctor who was hanging out there and eating everything in sight before going to prison.

He was a kindly 60ish general practitioner who had been convicted of performing abortions. We all agreed it was a hell of a lot better than a coat hanger in a back room but, it was a felony. They refused to ever take any money from him and told him that they would save his place at the bar. The room in the boarding house was very unique. In fact the whole house was unique. Our room was at the front of the house on the second floor and looked out over the cable car line. It had a small door in the wall that opened to a cupboard that opened to the elements and would keep our food cold there. It was handy. We kept bread, cheese, milk and fruit there, which saved us a lot of money. The closet was a huge walk in room with a shower at one end.

The shower head looked like it came out of Dracula's castle and the fixtures were of strange animals. It was tiled in a black and white pattern and the curtain looked like something that might have belonged to Vampira. My Goth friends would have loved it. It was a great shower. There was a door in the wall that had been fastened shut that lead into the next apartment inhabited by Larry G. from Coos Bay, Oregon. He was a happy-go-lucky gay guy who rarely spent the evening alone. The keyhole in the door was supposed to be blocked. But frequently we found that it had been poked open. I don't know why. I believe that Cathy may have been responsible for at least some of the poking as strange noises emanated from his quarters with some frequency. Our room, Larry's, and two others, shared a water closet. The others were occupied by a bookie and the Pennypacker family.

Mrs. Penneypacker—a tiny little elderly woman who spoke only German—had the interesting habit of wadding up currency and hiding it all over, including inside the toilet paper roll, in the writing tablet caddy on the rotary phone and in the stairwell. I am sure, in retrospect, she had some form of dementia. The first time we saw her doing this, we tried to talk to her, but she looked frightened and scurried back to her room. Since we always left our door open, before long, we would see her coming along again depositing her little wads of cash. After her door closed we went out and collected what she had hidden. We were really broke at the time. I was still not receiving my subs and quarters, Cathy was not working regularly and often we were hungry.

At the time, we saw it as a gift from the gods and dashed out to dinner at the Green Lantern. Strangely enough, we never felt guilty—just lucky—when we beat Larry to the money. The back of the house had a huge studio apartment with a full bath and a kitchen, occupied by Richard W. For some reason, after Larry used the water closet, it would frequently appear as though a monsoon had hit and Richard would let us use his bathroom. We knew little of the bookie. He was always on the phone. He was friendly enough. He'd wave when we went by, then he moved soon after we got there. The basement was occupied by a Mexican family that had 7 or 8 children including a wonderful 5-year-old named Max. Both of us liked children and seemed to attract them. Because Cathy didn't work regularly, he spent a lot of time in our room. The first floor contained the manager Lucretia Fitzgerald and frequently her sister Olympia.

The back part of the house belonged to a family with a couple of teenagers. Lucretia and her sister claimed to be part of the elite in San Francisco who had fallen on hard times. I think it was probably true because every afternoon she dressed to the nines and invited us down for cream sherry and cakes at tea time. In spite of the fact that her makeup looked like it was applied by a cross-eyed clown, she was a gracious and regal hostess. Lucretia had been in the hospital three years before with pneumonia—which she talked about every time she had to go upstairs—and we found her talking about this hysterically funny. This got appreciatively worse when a butch buddy of Richard's (lovely girl named Sean) moved into the bookies old room. There was a popular movie starring Shirley Temple.

In the film, one of the teenagers in the movie would wander through the house letting out this atrocious moan. It was our habit in the evening to gather in Richards's apartment and drink Tavola wine (98 cents a gallon). Invariably at some point in the evening Sean would go out in the hall and mimic the girl in the film which brought Lucretia running upstairs. Richards's apartment had a fire escape. We hid Sean there, while the rest of us sat there deadpan, swearing we had not heard a thing.

I should be ashamed of myself, but it still makes me giggle. Another event that put us all in hysterics happened when Cathy and I decided to go to the movies. She was very much into classic productions. I think she was trying to educate me, so off we went to see "Tales of Hoffman" at the Nob Hill Theatre. As it happened, we sat under one of the pale blue lights placed around the theatre. We were happily watching people cross the river Styx, when suddenly Cathy screamed and grabbed me. She was on my left.

She started babbling and climbing up my shoulder and pointing behind her.

I leaned forward to see what she was talking about and there was a very large man with a very large "member." He was placing a "safe" on the member in this glowing blue light. The whole thing was totally surreal. I said "Oh my god it's a horse!"

That brought Cathy back and she said "Jesus! All I'd be able to do would be to lean up against it and cry". We must have insulted him because he harrumphed threw his coat over himself and went to another part of the theatre. I know that because I heard squeals at various points. When we told our friends about this everyone about died laughing. He became "equine-man" and was a frequent butt of jokes.

The tenants on the third floor included old Mr. Cohan, and his caregiver, a retired female nurse, and Betty, a hooker, with a five-year-old daughter named Anna. After Cathy showed up, Billy moved upstairs to one of the other rooms – and Cathy helped her. Old Mr. Cohen and his nurse occupied one of the apartments on the third floor. She carried a huge carpet bag that contained enough medical supplies to fill an ambulance. I think she was prepared for anything from a splinter to open heart surgery.

However she had no answer to his major complaint. Mr. Cohen's testicles were the size of a grapefruit. When he went downstairs it was like Lucretia Fitzgerald, but in reverse, he moaned and whined on every step, "Oy, the family jewels!" "My poor jewels." and "Hitler should have such jewels."

He repeated these things as he went step to step. All the time, the nurse said such things as, "You can do it." "Buck up." And "Atta boy!" This didn't happen very often, but when it did, the callous and unfeeling side of youth made us laugh hysterically.

Anna frequently hung out in our room since her mother slept a lot during the day. She and Max were buddies. We frequently took them to the park or to play land at the park when we were feeling flush ala Mrs. Pennypacker. Betty liked us. She frequently sent Anna down to us if she had a client. We would pop her in the bed between us, feed her breakfast in the morning and then send her back to her mom. I even took her and Max swimming at the YWCA one Saturday afternoon—they were great kids.

One client beat the hell out of Betty. We had to call the ambulance for her. Welfare came and got Anna. We said we would keep her, but they wouldn't allow it. We never saw her again. Years later when I got my discharge, we tried to take Max with us. Even though his family always ignored him they wouldn't allow it. Life outside of the flats had three dimensions. One: 8-4 office job with the Marine Corp, two: the YMCA, and three: hanging out at the gay bars on Broadway on the weekends.

One thing about the Marine Corp was very much like any office work: Go to work. Finish, and come home. Probably the most interesting part of the job was getting and returning home. Since I still was not getting my subs and quarters, I walked frequently – from 100 Harrison, to the corner of Fillmore and Jackson. I loved that walk, especially up Sutter Street lined with stores selling antique jewelry. Walking up Gary Street took me past Tommy's Joint.

Where there was always a whole turkey and a ham turning on spits in the window. Because I was so broke, some of my most fervent dreams involved going there to eat. A year or so later, an affluent friend took Cathy and me there for lunch, it wasn't nearly as good as it looked. When the weather wasn't good, I mixed myself in with a crowd of people and slipped onto the cable car. I took either the one on California and Market or the one further down. Depending on where the most people were waiting. I clutched my dime in my hot little hand, but I rarely ever had to pay. Going to work was often more difficult as there were fewer people waiting but it took too long to walk in the rain.

Milestone 23

The YWCA was different because I only had to be there weekends at 1 PM. The walk was easy. Generally, I put on my suit, flipped on the lights, sat in my chair and chatted with the folks that came in to do a few laps. The other women lifeguards at the "Y" did not like to work on weekends and so if there were requests for private lessons, I got them. The same was true of special events like birthday parties or (in this case), a baptism. A local televangelist had collected a few devoted souls who wanted him to baptize them. A lifeguard was required any time people were using the pool, but in this instance I did not have to take my shoes off or put my bathing suit on.

I met too fair young ladies in floral, cotton, long sleeve dresses, their hair in buns, and helped them deposit their change of clothes in the dressing room. Shortly after I opened the doors for the short chubby minister in a three-piece suit and a tall slender young man in a work shirt and pants. They all looked very solemn. I was pretty much a pagan, and found the whole thing slightly ridiculous, but kept my mouth shut. I was wondering how he was going to affect this baptism without ruining his suit, when I realized he was carrying a set of shoulder-high waders. He chatted amiably to all of us for a few minutes and then climbed down the ladder. I must admit I was totally remiss not realizing what could happen, but my mind was distracted by plans of Cathy and I going out that night.

The man was no taller than I was, and the pool was four feet deep. The minute his feet hit the pool bottom, the water started pouring down inside his waders. Talk about shock and awe! He started acting like a frog with rabies, yelling, jumping about, and trying to get out of the water. While it surprised me, I also tried hard not to laugh. I knew he was getting off balance so I immediately jumped in and thought "oh, no! There goes another watch!"

If you're a lifeguard, regardless of what else is happening, someone will go under and you'll have to jump in wearing your watch. I knew if he sunk to the bottom, I wouldn't be able to lift him. So I yelled for the young man to join me in the water. We managed get the waders unhooked and together we pushed, prodded, begged and, threatened finally getting him up the ladder. This obviously, cancelled the baptisms. The man we'd just saved, said some very "unchristian" things on the way to the dressing room.

At least thanked and asked me what he could do to repay me. I suggested he replace my watch if he liked. Apparently he didn't like—I never saw him again. Everyone went their own way. The girls and the young man each had a change of clothes. The preacher didn't but I heard he hired a cab. I called Cathy to bring me a change of clothes and then we were off to Saturday night in the gay bars.

Milestone 24

Because of a lack of transportation we spent a lot of time on Broadway, at Mona's Candlelight and another of our favorite hang-outs, Twelve Adler. There were also two clubs featuring drag shows: Finocchio's and The Beige Room. Mother Finocchio did not like the gay girls and was very unwelcoming. My gay uncle took Cathy and I there one time, and tipped big, but Mother Finocchio still stood in the corner and glared at us. The queens there were very attractive. Little Hispanic Ray D.

Young was cute as a button. One of the blonde singers there was reputed to sing in one of the choirs in a big church in San Francisco and they never knew "she" was a he. The Beige Room was extremely gay friendly, no cover charge for us! They even sponsored a tea dance on Sunday afternoons for the gay community. I received the next step in my gay education at The Beige Room. I had never been to a drag show at the Beige room and didn't know what to expect.

Two or three of my friends took me to a show and asked me to guess which performers were men in drag, and which were the biological women. Generally, it was pretty easy to tell who the guys were except for one gorgeous auburn haired beauty named Laurie Night: she had the voice of an angel no question about her. Heh. I didn't know about lip-syncs. I was drooling and my friends asked if I would like to meet her. She came and sat beside me and we chatted. She was so sweet. I must have let her know about my crush.

She put her arm around me and said, "Oh honey, I'm a boy". She patted my arm and said consolingly: "Sweetie, you will get over it." Then she introduced me to her lover, George. She said, "We can become very good friends."

George said, looking at me, "She is cute—can we adopt her?"

Another shop on Broadway that cannot be overlooked is Mike's Pool Hall. It had a sandwich bar in the front and four chairs in the window by the sidewalk. In the back were 4 pool tables that were surrounded by little old Italian men who stared at us. Mike was the stereotypical short order cook—big, hairy and kind of scary. He made the best pastrami sandwiches in the known world and added a handful of pepperoncini's to every order. When he gave you the sandwich, he'd always stare deeply into your eyes and frequently gave you your money back. How did he know?

For a couple days around Thanksgiving and Christmas, he would make huge turkey dinners and serve them for free. On New Year's Day, it was free corned beef and cabbage and red beans and rice. Goddess! I loved that man! He was gruff and didn't talk much, and I don't know what his thing about lesbians was, but he sure did love the girls. He treated us like he wanted to take care of every one of us.

"Tommy's 12 Adler" was a combination of bars. The upstairs was a straight bar with stairs leading down to a gay bar that opened on 12 Adler Street. They didn't have shows there, but you could buy anything you wanted in the way of street drugs. We didn't go there much as we were not into drugs at all.

"Mona's Candlelight" was like a crazy gay novel all by itself. Mother Frenchie (the bartender) was a miniature version of Mike (and not that miniature at that). If any of the perverted men (commonly known as "fish queens") made a pass at any of the gay girls, Mike leaped over the bar like superman. Within 2 minutes the miscreant found himself on the sidewalk on his hands and knees and "86-ed" forever.

The body of the bar consisted of seats built out from each wall with tables, and more tables in the center. The left side was lovingly called "homo row". The right side was the "Grayline perch" – the section where people on the Grayline sightseeing tour sat. The deal was, if you kissed your girl when "Grayline" guests were there, the bar would give you free drinks. The waitress was a statuesque attractive butch named Joyce V. The three singers were Ann Dee – who hypnotized the audience with the song "Kiss of Fire", Sandy Scott – a woman who could pass as a man any time, and chubby Duke Derrell who billed herself as "the last of the red-hot mamas".

On off nights Duke Derrell went out in the neighborhood with her tambourine to raise money for "the church." Years later I heard that she actually opened one in San Jose, but I didn't see it with my own eyes. She took a shine to me in my 20-year-old innocence, but the things that she said to me were not particularly religious. The other inhabitant of the establishment was Joe the piano player. Joe was absolutely terrified of earthquakes. If there was the slightest quiver, he was up, running, with his suitcase, onto the nearest bus to Yreka, CA, where he'd stay until he was sure San Francisco wasn't going to fall into the bay.

Broadway was one of the best places to be on Halloween (or "Bitches Christmas", as gay people called it then. The streets were filled with drag queens. Not the least of these: Mother Frenchie, in a harem costume, leading his alligator. The alligator was about 4 feet long from tip to tail and lived in Mother Frenchie's bathtub. Such was my life on Broadway.

I should probably take a minute to explain some of the gay language used. Words were used in making contact with others as signifiers or to designate one's role. Surprisingly enough, one of the most secret of these words was "gay." It was used to covertly signify one's orientation to someone that you suspected of like mind.

For instance, you might say to a co-worker, "I am going out tonight to have a gay old time." If the other person answered, "Yeah, me too," and laughed, you knew you were on the wrong track. However, if they froze, looked at you slowly, and said, "Really?" Then you pursued it. Jail-time for being gay was a potential for all of us in the GLBTQ+ community.

You didn't have to even do anything else to merit an arrest. You could be sitting quietly in a bar, having a beer, touching no one, and the next thing you knew, you were arrested, put on a bus, and be on your way to jail. The busts often happened on a Friday or Saturday night. You were held until court opened on Monday morning. Your parents or employer would be notified that you were arrested for visiting a "house of ill-repute." The term originally meant whore-house, but in San Francisco, came to mean gay bar. People were frequently disowned by their families and lost their jobs as a result of these arrests and that sometimes lead to suicide.

Roles were very important and distinct. There was "Jeuneflip", a baby butch. "Dyke"- average alpha type, and "Butch" – a super tough girl- they often sported men's clothes and had "masculine" type jobs. On the other side were the femmes – some were "tomboys" or "lipstick lesbian" types. There was a saying, "todays trade is tomorrow's competition" which means today's femme is tomorrow's butch. It was also said – "there were no femmes after 40."

During this time, I was 100% tomboy, femme. I had no choice. Cathy was a total butch. She was half Native American and half Irish and had been raised on a game farm near Dexter New York. As a child, she had spent a great deal of time with her tribe, but as a young woman, she had danced ballet on Broadway in New York. She was so brilliant. And I was so impressed. She kept her toe shoes with her and occasionally danced for me. She painted strange things – like a little man inside the womb of a dinosaur. She could convince anyone that she spoke with she was an expert in their field even though she had not graduated high school.

She was a good lover and very demonstrative physically and financially when we had it to spare. After a few months I discovered that she had a violent streak. After 3 drinks, I was bound to get pounded. There was no place I could turn to for help without getting myself in a lot of trouble with the police. Things got better financially after Billy Piper got Cathy a delivery job. Three or four times a month, Billy gave her a sealed box. Cathy wrapped it like a gift and deliver it somewhere in the mission district. I never knew what was in the box. I never asked what was in the box but she got $50 for each delivery, and we needed it desperately.

Milestone 25

Things were going along just fine, and then one day, a fateful call came from North Carolina. It concerned a government agency called "Civilian Investigation Division," or "CID". They were a team of three or four persons that traveled from base to base, looking for "illegal activities." They were searching for people stealing and selling government equipment, dealing and using drugs, and most "evil" of all, being homosexual. I don't know what happened in the men's divisions, but in the women's division, they would send in a woman to hang out for a while. After two or three days, she would zero in on a couple of women that she thought were gay. I guess it was a form of "gadar", but quite a few of the gay women seemed obvious to me.

The CID crew would take a woman into a closed room and harangue her for 24-48 hours until she broke and named every gay person she knew. They repeated this process with anyone so named until they thought they had gotten the names of all the "evil" gay people on the base. At this point, all those so named would have the chevrons cut off their sleeves, and they received an "undesirable" discharge, and were taken—lock , stock and barrel—and dumped outside the main gate of the base. I knew a number of gay women who had planned on a career in the Corps, whose hearts were broken because of this treatment. The one redeeming fact about this was people did not generally ask women if they had been in service. So unless they were looking for a government position that required extensive personal background checks, they were less negatively affected than their male counterparts.

The phone call was from a friend who informed me that I had been named by two or three different people and that CID was slated to be coming to San Francisco in the next month. I did not want an undesirable discharge and so Cathy and I hit upon a way around it. She called the base and told them that I was having a nervous breakdown. They sent an ambulance after me, and by the time it arrived, I was shaking and crying and babbling about my mother and they couldn't understand me.

I was naturally scared and upset and I came off authentic. At the base infirmary, they gave me something to calm me down which I fought like crazy. I am sure my fear and adrenalin helped, but it was an Academy Award winning performance. Consequently, they gave me something else on top of the first sedatives.

This was gilding the lily so to speak, and the next thing I knew, I woke up in an ambulance on the way to Oak Knoll Naval Hospital and what was affectionately termed the "Lolo Haole" Ward (that means "crazy foreigners" to non-Hawaiian speakers). Basically, I slept the first 24 hours and then Sparrow took over as a tour guide. Sparrow showed me the way to the mess hall, the slop chute, and the bus stop. I asked her why I needed the bus stop.

She laughed and said "once the shrink talks to you, he'll see you're just here to get out and he'll cut you loose. I'm crazy, not stupid. You'll be able to leave on Wednesday morning after 8 a.m. You won't have to return until Monday morning at 8 a.m. I don't leave, cos I've got no place to go."

And sure enough, that's exactly what happened. Except that the shrink insisted that I wasn't gay, Andy he shrink said, "You're only using it to get out of the service".

On the ward was Gertrude, my roommate, a pregnant girl who they allowed to stay till her baby was born. Additionally, a number of people who wouldn't come out of their rooms and talk with the rest of us. At the other end on our ward was the alcohol ward and mainly housed male officers with alcohol issues. In the morning, we fought over the newspaper that had the new cartoon coming out called Snoopy. We all loved it but couldn't all be first to read it. We were on tenterhooks reading about the first set of Siamese twins who were joined at the head and were being separated. It saddened all of us when we learned one twin lived and one didn't. I told Cathy and she got a big kick out of it. She showed up on Wednesday in a suit and tie with a dozen roses and made a big deal of taking my arm and leading me out of the ward.

I spent about three months in the hospital before the discharge came through, but no one bothered me. I spent most of my time there helping the "Waves" calm the upset and suicidal patients ("the waves" are the nurses in the marines) I learned something very important there from my roommate. She was a very nice young woman who had taken a serious fall and had an epilepsy attack. Two or three times a month she had a seizure.

Once during a seizure, while we were trying to undress her, we pulled her pants down and she pulled them back up. I got frustrated and yelled, "Gertrude, let us get you undressed!" She mumbled something that sounded like "sorry" and started to help us even though she was still seizing. I gave her two or three orders out of curiosity and she attempted to respond to all of them. This helped me years later, when there was an epileptic child in my day nursery. One time in particular when I was coming back to the house with five children and a bunch of groceries, I was following Kyra with my arms full of groceries when her knees buckled and she fell down and started seizing.

In frustration I cried out, "Oh no, Kyra, not now!" She shook herself off, stood up and walked up the stairs into the house. She never had another seizure in my house, although she did have a few with her mother on the way home. I think it is interesting that the gods have seen fit to either bless me or teach me things that seem totally unnecessary but later, proved to be among the most important things in my life.

Just before Christmas, I finally received my medical discharge. Cathy and I packed up and immediately headed for Indiana. What a mistake. It never occurred to us to stay in California or more specifically, in San Francisco. In hindsight, it's what we should have done. The Marine Corps personnel said, "Here's your discharge, here is your severance pay, go home!"

And so, we did.

Milestone 26

We had every intention of hanging out a few weeks, getting our balance and heading back to San Francisco. As a matter of fact, it took seven years to get back. It seems all these doors kept opening and as an Aquarian, I had to go through. Most of the time, it was only a temporary situation that gave me ideas. Two or three times an idea occurred to me that I wanted to walk permanently on a particular path, but the universe shoved me on. The first door opened when my parents gave me a welcome-home party and invited my stepfather, Bill. He asked us what our plans were and when we had blank stares on our faces, he suggested a season in Florida. He explained that this time of year (January) Florida was full of New Englanders on vacation, and that it was possible for anyone to get a job instantly. He offered to drive us down, said we could stay with Helen, could work the season and have a fun time. With nothing better on tap, we thought it was a great idea and so we agreed.

There is a saying, that if you get Florida sand in your shoes once, you are bound to come back. I suppose that I already had sand in my shoes from the time I watched those kids in Orlando before I started college—and so it was fated. He agreed to pick us up in a few days, but when the time came, he called and said that "something had come up" and he couldn't make it. He said he didn't want to disappoint us and so he had bought us tickets to Miami, and all we had to do was get on the plane. It was a red-eye flight and we arrived in Miami at 3 a.m. Helen met us, but because she worked as a proof reader at the Miami Herald, she had to get back to work. She gave us hugs, keys, and directions and put us in a cab to her apartment.

When we got there, there was no Coca-Cola in the place and because I was addicted, we went back out and walked the neighborhood until we found some. Once we got the Cokes, we stuck them in the fridge and went to bed; it comforted me just knowing they were there. Helen had a small apartment with two twin beds. Cathy and I climbed into one of them and slept like the dead. Helen came home very early in the morning and told us that we could have used both beds until she got there. But I told her we were just fine and we had been. She then told us a nice story about some lesbians who had come on to her. I think she wanted me to come out to her, but I was too traumatized from the Marine Corps to do it.

The next day we took a jitney across the causeway to Miami Beach. We went in to the first restaurant we saw, The Crossroads, and told the waitress we were looking for work. She sent us back to a huge hairy guy, the owner, and he looked us over. He said, "Well, you're, walking, talking, and breathing, you are hired."

Cathy, always the practical one, asked him how much we would get paid. He laughed and said "You're in Florida, chick. Minimum wage is 10 cents an hour. You'll be working for tips. If you're good, you'll do fine, if you're not it's your own problem. If you want the job, pick up a couple uniforms from the room and show up here tomorrow at 3 o'clock.

We showed up and worked a 12-hour shift, 3 p.m. to 3 a.m. In a restaurant that kept us running from the second we walked onto the floor. There was never a slow time, first was when the movies let out; next when the bars let out at; and, finally when people got off work. Fortunately, we were still in great shape coming from the Marine Corp. The restaurant must have been designed by someone who absolutely hated wait staff. In the right front corner was a soda fountain and in the left front corner, behind the hostesses' station was a glass case full of cakes and cookies. A counter with stools ran half-way along the right wall. In the middle of the wall was a sandwich station that contained the ingredients for bagels and lox, etc.

This was a kosher-style restaurant. The rest of the wall was dominated by the waffle iron, chopped liver, and salad fixings. The left rear corner housed a cold case that held key lime pie, etc. We put the order in the kitchen door and then ran all over getting the parts to put the order together. Often in the evening after the movies, we had groups of seven-eight people and putting their orders together was a major undertaking. We were each in charge of four tables, and Cathy had assured me that she had waited tables at The Blackwater Inn in Watertown New York. It took about two hours for me to realize that she had never waited tables in her life.

I covered all four of my tables, two of hers and kept my eye on the other two of hers to help where needed. We needed this job. I had already come to the conclusion that "truth" in Cathy's world was something twisted, changed, and hammered into whatever shape you wanted at the time. After living with Billy Piper and hanging out on Broadway I'd discovered that truth was not something some gay folk cared much for. Truth was uncomfortable at the least and life threatening at worst for gays. I also decided that the majority of people lied in order to get approval or out of fear. Therefore, I reasoned, one should accept it. My first trainer in this area of truth and lies was my mother who, while not gay , was certainly a good liar. It worked very well with Cathy because she was a consummate liar of the first degree.

This stood me in good stead with Cathy, since I often listened to Cathy talk to a new acquaintance and convince them she was an expert in their field, regardless of what the field was. She could be talking about animal husbandry, French cooking, or nuclear science. It didn't matter. Within a week, Cathy had the workings of a waitress down pat. No one could question her intelligence. She was one of the best-read and erudite people I have ever known, it didn't matter she'd never graduated high school. This seems to be a pattern with me. I am not seriously attracted to beautiful bodies or gorgeous looks, it's intelligence and wit that turns me on. Cathy certainly had that and I shined it on when she slipped into one of her fantasy personalities. Not much happened in Florida, we worked 12 hours a day, six days a week, with one day off for the beach the whole three months we were there.

We lived in my mother's apartment building which had a long breezeway in the middle. Cathy had just taken the garbage out when I heard, some yelling, "No! No! Stop! No! Don't!"

I ran out to see what was wrong and was confronted with a tenant holding a rifle, pointing it at the garage floor. Cathy looked terrified and kept exhorting the man to stop as she pointed to something in the same direction. Then I saw it, a huge hairy black tarantula.

Cathy yelled "Don't shoot, I've got this!" Then she took off toward the spider in a grand jete'. She flew as graceful as a bird and landed squarely on top of the unfortunate tarantula, which splattered in every direction. Cathy turned to the offending tenant and said, "You are an absolute idiot! If you had shot, the bullet would have shattered or ricocheted and gone in any of sixteen directions and killing who-knows- what. Besides that, that spider had as much right to be here as you do and if you feel that way about them, you should move to Wisconsin".

The other event of note happened on a Monday around 4 a.m. when we had just come home from work. Cathy looked out the window and screeched – "Get the hell out of here!" I looked out the window and there was an ordinary middle aged man, busily masturbating while looking in our window. Cathy grabbed a tennis racket that was by the door and ran out after him but he jumped in his car and drove away quickly. The same thing happened the following Monday night, and though we ran immediately to the car we'd bought from our tips (we bought it from one of Helen's boyfriends), we couldn't catch the peeping tom. We drove straight to the police station.

When we told the cops what had happened, they looked at each other, snickered, and in unison said, "Slippery John."

They said he had been haunting that neighborhood for months. They theorized he followed waitresses (many of whom worked late) home. He often went back to the same place a number of times and though they had set traps, they had never been able to catch him.

About this same time, another of the waitresses told us that she was leaving to go work Mardi Gras in New Orleans. The season generally ended with Passover and then the tips would fall way down. She invited us to come with her, and we said sure, so we all packed and bundled into our car and off we went. Mardi Gras was absolute chaos - swarms of people (mostly half drunk), and everyone partying all the time. I managed to eat more Jambalaya and poor boy sandwiches than you can shake a stick at. We haunted the French Quarter, "Vieux Carre," bought protection charms and even rode the streetcar named "Desire". After two weeks, we took our gains and headed back to Florida. We spent a weekend with Helen, and on an early Monday morning, we headed toward New York.

Although she had lied about knowing how to drive a stick shift, by the time we left Miami, Cathy was driving. About the middle of the morning the usual Florida rainstorm hit and became acquainted with the issues our little car had to offer. It was a coupe with wing windows on each side, and in some way the rain managed to get through them and sprinkle us. The windshield wipers made a buzzing noise, but wouldn't move unless I hit the window with my fist. If it rained hard, I hit fast; if it rained slower, I slowed down.

I got good at it, but my hand got pretty sore too. In the middle of the afternoon the sun came out and though it was cool it was still a lovely day. And as if on cue, by full dark the headlights, tail lights, interior and dash lights went out. We were on a two lane highway with swamp on both sides and no place to pull off. Cathy said that we didn't dare stop as someone might ram us, and we were each hanging out the windows on both sides making sure we didn't drive into the swamp. Cathy said, "oh shit, there is a car coming behind us. Use the flashlight to shine out the back window so they will see us."

The car whipped around us, slowed down and flashed its lights. "Oh thank god, they want us to follow them." Cathy breathed and immediately moved ahead.

We drove about two miles when we saw another car coming behind us and I flashed the flashlight. That car passed us, slowed down, then dropped behind us. Tucked safely between these two cars we drove the last few miles into Ocala, Florida. As we reached a garage, the first car flashed its lights and took off. As we pulled over, the second car honked, and the driver waved and kept going. We never even got to thank them but we certainly blessed their names. Once again, Cathy portrayed herself as an expert and said her brother had taught her all about cars. As it happened, she did know what she was doing as she took the generator apart and did something arcane with some objects called brushes. Whatever she did, it worked. The guys in the garage told us that our breather pipe was totally clogged with thick oil and needed to be burned out which would take an hour.

They told us that there was a bed and breakfast three doors down and because we had made quite a bit of money in New Orleans, we went down and spent the night. The next day we made it all the way to Charleston with no problems. We decided to save money and sleep in the car. We pulled into a gas station, next to some cars waiting for service. Two people sleeping in a coupe is not good. We left early the next morning and that night reached Chesapeake Bay. We decided to take the ferry across that night instead of waiting for morning, the ride was longer than we thought and by the time that we made it across and got going, it was the middle of the night.

We stopped at a diner, hoping food would give us a shot of energy, the fry cook was another large, hairy and slightly scary guy.

Cathy and I were wearing Hawaiian shirts we'd bought in Florida. We cracked up when he said, a big grin crossing his face, "I'll wrestle ya for that shirt."

I liked that line so well it became one of my stock phrases. I must have used it at least a thousand times over the years. He also said, "You chicks look exhausted, I got a van out back, here's the key, nobody will bother you—go sleep." And we did. The next morning, when we went in to give him the key, he insisted we sit down and have breakfast.

He fixed bacon, eggs, potatoes, pancakes and orange juice. We couldn't finish it all and so he packaged the rest and refused to take any money as he sent us on our way. We made it to the New Jersey turnpike in the middle of the day when the car started overheating. It turned out that there were tiny holes in one of the hoses.

Cathy jury-rigged it with adhesive tape and refilled the radiator one coke-bottle-at-a-time from the water she fished from a ditch. We were not using a map as Cathy said that she knew the way, we were going up the Palisades Highway toward Watertown. As it happened, she was wrong, very wrong and by the time we realized that, we were on the Storm King Highway and way too far up. That road earns its name honestly and we were in near 'white-out' conditions just before we hit Nyack, New York. We stopped at the first sign of a hotel which also turned out to be full of truckers evading the storm. The doors lead through a bar which was full and noisy. We each got two or three propositions before we made it to the desk and the room upstairs. It was still noisy, but we were both wiped out and cold in our Hawaiian shirts.

We were asleep in minutes and woke to a very cold day and decided to get in our car and find a place to have breakfast only to discover that we had four flat tires. Our little Florida car could not cope with the Adirondack ice and snow of an east coast winter. We found someone to fix the tires while we had breakfast and before the middle of the afternoon, we pulled into the side yard of Cathy's home. Cathy's brother, Graydon, was dabbing something onto a piece of cotton that was tied to the back door screen. Cathy had not been home in three years. Graydon looked up and said of the cotton, "Don't suck on it, it's deadly poison."

Then he walked into the kitchen. They had a very strange family dynamic. Her sister-in-law and 7-year-old niece came out to greet us. Cathy's room had not been touched since she'd left. We stayed there about three weeks. Her home was near a small town named Dexter and not far from Watertown, New York. Cathy had been active in little theatre and introduced me to her best bud, Charles Peirce, who was home visiting. Charlie introduced himself as "the world's most famous male actress—as yet undiscovered." He had just returned from a semester in California at the Pasadena Playhouse.

He was planning to leave for San Francisco soon and urged us to go with him. We explained to him that we very much wanted to join him, but we needed to replenish our funds and were looking for jobs. One day, Cathy, me, Charles and a young man named Maurice took a picnic on south lakes beach on Lake Erie. Though dressed in a white shirt and white shorts, Charles went through his entire repertoire of "funny ladies", imitating Tallulah Bankhead, Carol Channing, Bette Davis and Rosalind Russell. It was the funniest thing I had ever seen. Later he became the toast of the gay nightclubs in San Francisco.

Try as we might, we couldn't find a job in the area, and grabbed what we had and headed out to Indiana. I knew we could stay with my parents and that they had invested in a Dairy Queen-type franchise, called "Dairy Treat" where we could work. We also signed up for a program called "Fifty-two Twenty" that was established to help veterans reestablish themselves back into civilian life. We'd each get $20 dollars a week, until we got work. My parents were giving us room and board and 25 cents an hour, thinking that was enough under the circumstances. My mother, never an easy person to get along with, was passive aggressive towards Cathy.

Someone told us that RCA Victor, only 18 miles north of us, in Indianapolis, was hiring. When we went there, we were immediately hired for the graveyard shift to make records.

Our position required us to stand next to a 2x3' grill that heated square pieces of vinyl. When the vinyl reached the right temperature, we plopped them into a machine not unlike a waffle iron and pushed two catches to cook it. Standing for 8 hours with only two breaks and a short lunch was not fun. We got home to bed at about 8 a.m. By noon, my mother was yelling at us to get up for lunch.

I remember my mother saying, "what do you think this is a hotel?" I got up as a rule, but let Cathy sleep. My dad said, "Ruth, she's only been asleep four hours. For god's sake! She worked all last night." My mother's response was, "I fixed a meal at noon and I expect people to eat."

By the weekend, I was exhausted. As it happened, my parents went to their cabin on the river where they spent most weekends in the summer. Actually their country home was much nicer than the mosquito-ridden place where their cabin was located. But the three other cabins around them held some of their best friends and so they spent their weekends playing Canasta and eating fried chicken and turtle. Cathy and I used the weekend to find a tiny egg-shaped trailer in a mobile home park in our home town. It was tiny. There was a couch at one end and a breakfast nook at the other with a sink, stove and refrigerator in the middle. The communal toilet and bathroom was about 25 yards away, but it was paradise after living with my mother. Although we left a note, I felt we needed to speak to her in person. So before we left for work Monday, we went out to see her. She was watching the Dodgers on their small TV and crocheting when we got there.

Instead of commenting on our move, the first thing she said was; "Do you think that this relationship between you and Cathy is healthy?"

For once in my life, I said exactly the right thing. "I haven't had a cold in six months," I quipped. Cathy snorted and went flying out the door.

My mother sneered and said "I always did think you were a little queer."

I turned and walked out the door. Cathy was laughing so hard in the car she nearly wet herself. The ride to work was a merry one. We went to RCA and told them that we simply could not do the record job. They moved us to the 3 p.m. to 11 p.m. shift, where we sat and made television tubes. We worked there a few years and then in 1955 we quit. It was hot, dirty and exhausting work. By this time, we had bought a much larger trailer and were renting space in someone's backyard. We supplemented what we could buy with catfish, croppy, and bluegills. My father had a large garden which we had access to also.

The first weekend we had off, we visited my Aunt Helen (not my mother). She was the wife of my father's youngest brother. They had been married when he was in the army and stationed in Saint Louis. I liked her best of all the relatives on that side of the family. One afternoon, sitting on her porch, a tenant, who rented the small apartment upstairs, came in with a little baby. She was a 16-year-old with a screaming six-week old baby boy.

She said, "if he don't shut up soon, I'm going to dump him in the nearest garbage can."

I said, "Give me that baby." I'd spent most of my teen years baby-sitting; I knew how to deal with crying kids. When I took him, his little belly was as hard as a rock from gas. I laid him face down across my knees and started bouncing my feet. Immediately he started like a little motorboat taking off across the river. Within a few minutes the baby farts and the tears stopped. I picked him up, laid him across my shoulder and he fell instantly to sleep. The poor little man was exhausted.

Covela (his mother) said "Will you please take care of him?"

By this time Cathy was working at the local sewing machine store, sewing and teaching, and I worked at the local American Legion hall when they catered events. Covela worked in a local bank and offered me ten dollars a week, and since I worked mostly at night, I took the job. I took care of Ricky Lee in her apartment for the first two or three weeks, and then, since it was okay with Covela and her husband Mac, we shoved a crib into our tiny bedroom and kept him all week. Covela had him on weekends and Cathy watched him at night. It limited Cathy and my sex life to weekends, but it had deteriorated to that anyway. After about two years, Covela got pregnant again and decided to stop working, and to take Ricky back. It broke my heart.

Milestone 27

Since I now needed a job, I was perusing the wanted section in the paper and found an ad for a waterfront director at a scout camp not far away. Since I was not only a water safety instructor but also had received the rank of instructor–trainer while working in the YWCA, they were glad to have me. It required me living for 10 weeks at a camp 60 miles away from home, Cathy was not at all happy. I only got 2-3 weekends off the whole summer and since we only had the one car, she would not be able to come visit me. Actually I was glad to get away because we had been living mostly on the fish we caught and our relationship had deteriorated since some of her violent tendencies had shown up. There was no one I could talk to and I simply had to defend myself against her when she got angry.

Life at the camp was wonderful. I shared a cabin with three young women in their late teens. I was 24 and having a ball. It was great - wonderful food I didn't have to cook or clean up after, a lovely warm river to swim in and great kids to teach. I had an assistant, Nancy, a college student at Indiana University who obviously developed a flaming crush on me in the first few days. It was flattering. She was cute and had a gorgeous voice being an opera major at the university. Our nicknames were Doc and Paddles. The three girls in my cabin were Drano, Babo and Ajax. Ajax was 17, 5 ft. 8 inches with dark auburn hair. She was clever, witty and very smart.

Before long at night, she was slipping over and snuggling in my bed. That scared the crap out of me because obviously, she was jail bait. In the evenings when we were not on duty, we took a canoe up the river to a secluded spot and made out. Nancy also talked me into going up to the secluded spot with tents, cots, etc. I found myself making out with Nancy because I was afraid that she would tell someone if I didn't, but my heart longed for Ajax. She turned 18 on the 1st of July and over the Fourth (when we had a four-day weekend, she and I went to Cincinnati), by now I was head over heels in love with her and begging her to come away with me. She had plans to go to Indiana State in the fall and refused to consider anything else. She said we could be together on weekends and after graduation we would be together.

I decided since I had the GI bill and two years left to graduate, I would go to college too. One night there was a sleep over planned out on the hill with all the scout campers. The unit was empty and Ajax and I were in one of the tents making out when Babo showed up unexpectedly. She took off at a dead run. I rearranged my clothes and took off after her to try to explain. I chased her all the way to the main house which held the office infirmary.

She locked herself in the bathroom and no matter how much I begged and pleaded she would not come out. She was one of those religious, sanctimonious types and I knew she would never understand. I begged her not to do anything to hurt Ajax, but I knew she would go to the director. We only had two more weeks of camp and my only hope was that the director (who was obviously a lesbian) would do nothing. And that is exactly what happened. We heard nothing about it.

When I went home, I talked Ajax into going with me as I didn't want to face Cathy alone. When we got there, I told Cathy that we were over, that I was going back to college and I was in love with Ajax. Ajax and I spent the rest of the time at my parents' river front cabin until it was time for her to go home and get ready for school. Cathy went to New York at this time and so I went over and got our two cats and moved in with my parents. At the university, I signed up as a speech major and got a part time job at the nursery. I spent most of my time driving back and forth between Indiana and Ajax's school in Missouri.

Cathy would often call me in the middle of the night. Considering she was calling me in Missouri from New York, meant it was an even later time of night for her. Cathy pled and cried, begging me to come back to her. At the same time, Ajax was withdrawing more and more from me. She had joined a sorority and didn't want to be seen with me much. I read the handwriting on the wall and saw she was just a kid getting started and didn't want the ties that came with me.

Milestone 28

One spring evening when Cathy called, she said she was in my home town, on her way to California and she wanted to say goodbye. I told her, fine and went out to meet her. We drove to the creek where we used to fish, she parked and pulled out a 45 caliber hand gun.

She told me nobody left her like that, and that I should definitely say my goodbyes now. In college I had been in drama classes and working with the plays we put on. I think that was what saved my life.

I said, "Oh honey, you really do love me! I wasn't sure. I love you too!" I planted a big wet kiss on her. She looked startled and awkward, dropped the gun, and proceeded to make love to me right there. It was all pretty awkward and what she thought was me shaking with passion was actually me being scared shitless.

Afterwards, we agreed she would stay and go to Indianapolis and get a job and a place to live. I would keep my job, stay in school and join her when I could. So I finished that semester, and because I was at a small Baptist college that required a class in religion, I decided I would take it someplace else. I quit my job and moved to Indianapolis to the apartment Cathy and I had found. I ran into my old friend, Bobby Buckner, on the street in Indianapolis and he told me about this apartment.

It was on Delaware street, across from the John Herron Art Institute. The upstairs held three apartments, ours and two apartments belonging to a couple of older gay men. Bobby had a small apartment downstairs on the side of the main house. The main house was inhabited by Mother Mitchell, a chubby old queen in his 50s. He liked nothing better than to cook sauce for three days and then throw huge spaghetti dinners for all of us. This came in handy because while Cathy was working at Western Union, I had quit my job and we were a bit on the poor side. One of the gay guys upstairs, affectionately known as Aunt Louise, was a line worker at the local automobile plant.

Once when I was in his apartment I noticed there was a Silver Star medal in a frame on his table. I knew that people were only awarded the Silver Star for doing something extraordinary in service. I asked him how he got it and he broke into giggles. He said he kept it there to remind himself of an extraordinary person he once met.

He related. "It was during the Battle of the Bulge when we were all hunkered down freezing to death. The Americans had a ton of medicine but the food trucks were having trouble getting to us so we had damn little food. On the other side the Germans had tons of food but no medical supplies – I don't know who figured this out. The first thing I knew was when they were looking for a volunteer to go stand with the German soldier as mutual hostages during an exchange of food and medicine. I found myself on the edge of the forest with a Teutonic god as my fellow hostage. He was unbelievably beautiful, and we found some interesting ways to spend our hour together. We had two more exchanges of food and medicine and we both insisted on being the hostage for our respective sides each time. When the war was over and the Allies were in Germany, I searched for him in the town he said he was from but found no sign of him. I assume he didn't make it back. And I've never felt that way about anyone since." Cathy and I lived there for a year and became the "token dates" for whenever their companies had parties, etc. That summer, I enrolled in Butler University and took the religion and botany classes I needed.

Milestone 29

I graduated from college and was offered a job at a newspaper. It was a small throw-away paper located on the east side of Indianapolis. The minute I took the job, the woman who'd worked there for two years as the typist and type setter, quit. She left me with duties to find and gather the news, as well as lay out the paper, sell advertising and create the ads. It was just too much. I lasted about three months. The only good thing about it was that I got to hire my cousin Paul as a paperboy. He was born on my 14th birthday and was always my favorite. Years later he told me that he kept the job till he was 16. The publisher, who also published "The Indiana Catholic and Record" (an Archdiocese Newspaper), owned the paper I worked on.

The publisher realized it was too much for me and suggested I go to the Catholic paper. The priest/editor, one Father Bossler, interviewed me, and hired me to do advertising. This is known in the news trade as selling the blue sky. Because you are trying to tell a bunch of hard-headed business men that by advertising in your paper, they will get more business. As nearly as I could tell this was all a bunch of crap and rarely did anything for anybody. Father Bossler had a pretty complete list of all the Catholic business men in the surrounding area. He would give me a list of names, locations and the church each person belonged to, and would send me out to meet and convince these people into taking an ad.

While I was pretty successful at it I couldn't escape the niggling feeling that it was a bit like blackmail. Although I'd officially gotten over what I call my "Catholic period" with Jud, this experience made the religion even more distasteful to me. I was already on the verge of quitting the paper when he told me that he had hired an assistant and wanted me to train him. It turned out that the guy had been a milk man and had no experience with any kind of publication. He had lost his job, and being a good Catholic, had asked for help, and so they hired him. I decided to go along with the plan and help train him before I left. It was was rather like teaching a monkey to write poetry. The new guy probably had a third grade spelling ability and couldn't even begin to conceive of or lay out an ad. I told Father Bossler that the guy was never going to be able to do this job at the end of a month when I went to pick up our checks.

He said, "Oh well, you can help him, just take him with you and let him drive." Then he handed me our checks.

I glanced at the checks and as usual, mine was $350. I nearly fainted when I saw that my "assistant's" was $700. I said, "Wait, there is a mistake here, this says $700."

Father Bossler said, "No mistake; that is his salary."

I said, "What do you mean?! He is doing nothing, and is getting twice what I get."

He said, "But you must understand, he has seven children."

I was seeing red, and said, "So you are saying that if I had fucked more, I would get more money?"

He replied, indignantly, "How dare you speak that way to me!"

I said, "I won't speak to you at all – I quit!"

Milestone 30

Back to the old drawing board. My next job I was docent at the Children's Museum in Indianapolis. The director, Grace Golden really liked and hired me; even though I didn't have a background in anthropology or archaeology. She told me she wanted me to take over for her in years to come when she retired. She gave me books to read and assigned chapters to read and then we'd discuss them an hour each day. The museum was situated in an area that had once been fine homes. It was in a beautiful three-story Georgian home with each room dedicated to a different time period. I loved the museum with all my heart.

I loved setting up the displays and loved leading tours of the children who came to visit. I loved our "pet" Glyptodon and all the other creatures from the Pleistocene epoch. Over the years the area we were located had changed demographics and had become mostly African American. Because of this, frequently black neighborhood children would come in to walk around the museum. When this happened, Grace Golden would assign one of us to follow them around to "insure" that they "would not steal or damage anything". We had two people in their 50s and 60s serving as housekeepers - one male and one female, both black. Grace referred to them as "the girl" and "the boy". Grace was very, very prejudiced. During this same time, Cathy and I had become close friends with Rena Sands, a young black woman who sang at a local bar.

We had been to her home for meals, she had been to ours, and we'd gotten to know her family. During that time, she became pregnant and eventually delivered a beautiful little boy. His name was Tyrone and I got to be his godmother. Tyrone's father, while he loved Rena very much, was a Greek-American who knew that his family would never accept him marrying a black woman. This was in 1957. Rosa Parks refused to give up her seat to a white man in 1955. Segregated water fountains were abolished in 1964. Prejudice was endemic in society. Along about the time that Tyrone was 18 months, Rena got fed up with the situation between her and her man and decided to go to California to stay with her cousins and start over.

Because it was the end of the month and a week before she was leaving, she gave up her apartment and moved in with us temporarily. The day she was leaving, I picked her up to take her to the bus station downtown. I did this on my lunch break but confided in a coworker and asked her to cover 15- 20 minutes if I was late. I had forgotten how jealous she was of me and didn't even think she would go to the director.

Not only did she tell the director I might be late, she also told her I'd be late because of a black woman. Grace Golden called me in and told me that she could not keep someone with such a lack of judgement and values on her staff, and fired me on the spot. It broke my heart.

Many years later, I took my own children back just to see the place. It had expanded and Grace Golden had died. The bitch co-worker that told Grace about me and who was jealous was now the director; I only hope that all her displays went crooked and the Glyptodon bit her. I was so devastated when Grace fired me that I didn't know which way to turn and Cathy decided that something had to be done. She reminded me that when I was in college that I'd wanted to teach at an Indian school in Arizona.

Milestone 31

Two of our best buddies Dick and Steve had lived in Arizona for a while and loved it. They told us about a lesbian friend of theirs who owned a gay bar, the Happy Landing, in south Phoenix. We said the hell with it. We loaded up the car and the little Pontoon boat we had purchased the year before with our two cats, one dog and all the possessions we could. My mother fried up a mess of fried chicken and made concentrated iced tea in a thermos that we could thin with water along the way, and off we went.

After many breakdowns and problems, we arrived in Phoenix. We found a little motel almost across the street from the Happy Landing and rented a cottage there. It was about one step up from a dirt floor, Hogan, but we figured it would do till we got settled. The two lesbians who owned the bar (Kay – a big white haired "stomper") and June (Kay's good-looking young lover) were extremely friendly. They remembered Steve and Dick and liked them, so we got the royal treatment; they took us out to dinner, let us use their swimming pool, and generally made much of us.

Immediately I signed up to be a substitute teacher. I couldn't get a teaching license before taking a class in Arizona history. Cathy went to work at a restaurant owned by some of Kay's friends. I waited and waited and when I never got a call for substitute teaching, I went back to the office. They were apologetic but explained that since they had no real flu season that year and since they had a number of regular subs, they hadn't gotten around to calling me.

About that time Rena and her Greek boyfriend and their boy Tyrone, showed up on their way back to Indiana. He had come to California, married her and said that as far as his family was concerned, they could lump it. When they left, Rena raved about how great California had been. Cathy looked at me and I looked at her and two days later, we were in Oakland, CA.

Milestone 32

We went to my uncle's bar, but because it was the weekend and he was very busy, he recommended a little motel down the street. The cockroaches there were even bigger than the ones in Phoenix, but since the cats liked to play with them and I suspect, ate a few, all was not lost. Since it was close to Thanksgiving, we went off to the unemployment office to see what we could find. There were a number of temporary jobs available, which we were glad to accept. We knew that we would be moving to San Francisco at the first opportunity. We both loved San Francisco and felt it was our true home.

But I got a job in the toy department of Montgomery Ward, while Cathy got a job mailing out gifts for some big corporate outfit. She did a lot of work with Mission PAC and we both fell in love with it. I sent some of the wonderful candied fruit to my mother and Cathy sent a selection of fruit and candy to her brother's family. I really liked the job in the toy department. Everything was so cheerful. The majority of the women worked on commission there so I spent a lot of time setting up displays and cleaning up. I never approached a customer if there was a commissioned employee there to wait on them. As a result, the women there liked me a lot and at the end of the temporary job they offered me a full time employment.

The other thing that happened there was I met another lesbian. She was a temporary employee and an art teacher in Oakland. She had seen Cathy, very butch-looking, and approached me the day after. She was funny, friendly, and talented. We became fast friends, which lasted until she retired and returned to Oklahoma. Just as Kentuckians come to Indiana for a better life, Okies came to California during the dust bowl. You can hardly find someone in California who is not descended from or related to those Okies who fled the dustbowl in the 1930s.

I didn't take the job because I had my eye on a job in San Francisco. Cathy and I had made enough money for our move to San Francisco. On New Year's Day, Cathy and I went to our old apartments, Fitz's Flats, to see our old friend Richard Mayfield. Except for Richard's space, we found that it had been turned into a half-way house for developmentally delayed people. We stayed for his New Year's Day party and it turned out that a lot of champagne and a ton of spaghetti do not work well together.

To this day, I have never liked champagne, draw your own conclusions. In the next few days we found a little cottage on Masonic Ave in San Francisco. It was one of the cottages built right after the 1906 earthquake to house people who were living in the parks and on the streets. The landlady lived in a converted building behind it and was nutty as a fruitcake. When we paid her rent she turned around and threw all the bills into the floor of her closet, which was covered with money. It is a good thing we were not larcenists.

The cottage had a small backyard and raspberry bushes by the fence. One day while sitting out there and nibbling raspberries a voice floated over the fence. He said, "hey you two, you all look like my kind of people, come over here and meet me."

It turned out he was a drag queen from Texas named Gene. He performed in boots, short shorts, a vest, and a belt with two play guns – Two Gun Tessie. He was blonde, chubby, and funny as a cow on a crutch. He invited us for dinner and put so much food on the plates that Cathy and I each took enough leftover food home we could eat three more meals. We became very close friends with Gene and his partner. He even invited us to see his drag show on Broadway a couple of times.

My best friends always seem to be gay men, I get them and they get me, and we get along beautifully. It's probably the purest kind of friendship one can have—neither one is interested in the other sexually, nor in our respective partners. The friendship is simply that and wonderful.

Milestone 33

Gene told us about a lesbian bar down in the Haight district called the, Who Cares. Cathy and I decided to go the coming Saturday night and got there early enough to claim two bar stools. That was great because by 9:30 it was wall-to-wall dykes. I knew that San Francisco was supposed to be the capital of the gay community; I had no idea there were that many lesbians in the world.

I'm tiny-of-bladder and there came a time when I had to try to get to the ladies' room. I am only 5' 2" and soon was engulfed in a sea of humanity. I was near panic when this tall slender butch stepped up and said, "you trying to get to the John?"

I nodded and she took my hand and led me into the middle of the crowd. With an excuse me here and a watch it there, and with deft application of her sharp elbows, she quickly led me to the door of the John. When I came out, she was waiting for me and very quickly led me back to my bar stool. About that time, the stool next to Cathy became available.

She hopped onto it and said, "Hi, I'm Marti, and I've never met you guys before."

Cathy, who had been a bit uptight when she saw Marti walking with me, soon relaxed and they hit it off right away. I was getting nervous because Cathy was on her third drink, which meant that sooner or later that night, I was going to get smacked around. As it happened, when it was time to go, Marti talked Cathy into going to The Happy Boy for a hamburger.

Thank the fates, whenever Cathy ate enough to sober up some, I didn't get punched out. Marti became our best buddy and Happy Boy became our place. I had no idea at the time how important she was. Or that everything significant that happened to me from that point onward, came directly from her. A few weeks later she told us about a Sunday Brunch at the Who Cares and we went down to meet her.

She was sitting with two friends that she introduced us to. She explained that they were having at least one house party a month on a Saturday night, because too many bars were getting busted. You could still be sitting in a legal bar, having a legal beer, touching no one and be arrested for visiting a house of ill repute. They would choose a gay bar, usually a men's bar, and come around late on a Saturday night with greyhound buses. They would load up everyone who didn't manage to run away or hide and take them to jail to spend time in the drunk tank.

Because it was the weekend, people were not able to hire a lawyer, make bail or get out in any way til Monday morning court. They would ascertain the names addresses and places of employment of the people they arrested. They would then contact the families and their jobs and explain that they had been arrested for visiting a house of ill repute and the cops would make it clear that they had been arrested in a gay bar. The term was originally coined to mean a whore house but the police happily tarred us with the same brush.

Some families rejected their gay members and many places fired their gay employees. Marti's friends, Del Martin and Phyllis Lyon, who later became well-known activists for GLBT rights, were just starting their little club. They invited us to join and Cathy and I became among the first Daughters of Bilitis or the DOB. The parties were held in Del and Phil's house. It was a welcoming little house at the top of Castro Street on Red Rock Hill. They had bought it for $7000 and it had a view from the bay bridge to the golden gate.

We soon started "rap sessions" on a monthly basis. That was when a whole group got together and took one subject and kicked it around for a couple hours. In one session, we discussed infidelity and I noticed a woman leading a small cute dark woman around the circle, finding a place to sit. She was leading the smaller woman carefully thru the maze of bodies. I commented to Cathy, "I don't think that woman sees well."

Later when we were drinking tea and coffee and standing around in groups, I asked Marti about her. She said, "oh that's Dubbi – she's a Creole from Louisiana. She looks like a kid but is actually 21 and a student at San Francisco State."

I asked, are they a couple? She doesn't seem to see very well."

"No they are just friends and she is totally blind."

I said, "Oh, does she have a dog?"

Marti said, "No, she goes everywhere on a cane and nothing slows her down."

About that time Dubbi and her friend came over to the coffee table and Marti introduced us. I was immediately taken with her. She had such a great smile and a good way about her.

After we met Del, he started a magazine called "The Ladder" which we mailed all over the country. For one of the rap sessions, they invited a man, Jess Stern, who was writing a book about lesbians. The book, "The Grapevine," is still available. I remember it was a fun session. He asked how often lesbians have sex. One of our members quipped, "when you get involved with DOB and "The Ladder," there's no longer any time for that."

Although many of the members of the DOB were closeted due to jobs and family, we decided to get involved in the election process. We invited the current crop of local candidates to a coffee session. Only one had the courage to show up, and thereby earned our undying loyalty and support. Her name was Diane Feinstein. She asked many interesting questions and became a lifelong supporter of the GLBT. As the DOB expanded we developed three more chapters, Los Angeles, Philadelphia and Chicago. In the mid-60s we had two national conventions, one in Los Angeles and one in San Francisco that were great fun.

Since we were established in our jobs, shortly after meeting Marti, we moved to a larger unfurnished apartment. It had a view of the whole city and we furnished it our way. Marti moved in across the hall, and spent most of her time at our place. At one time, one of Marti's ex-girlfriends who was teaching school down south, came up to spend a couple of weeks. We had them over for dinner and at one point when Lois and I were doing dishes, she asked me my sign. I said Aquarius, and she said, oh no, I'm a Leo, we are opposites, we will never get along.

"That's a bunch of crap," I said.

She said, "Oh really, are you educated in astrology?"

I said, "Of course not!"

"Then you are hardly qualified to speak,"she retorted.

This pissed me off, and I decided I was going to show her. The next day we went to a book store looking for books on astrology. The owner said that if we wanted to do horoscopes, then we would also need an ephemeris. Using that, with the information from the book, I managed to construct both Cathy's chart and my own. In the back of the book it described what other aspects meant. As I went through them, I started laughing when I discovered that one person's Saturn to another's Uranus was called the Murders sign. But as I thought about it, I had realized that Cathy had already made at least one attempt in that direction and so I laughed it off. The more I played with Astrology, the more I realized that there was something to it, but at that time, it never occurred to me that it would become one of my most lucrative professions.

DOB saved my life in a couple of ways. One Sunday afternoon, something upset Cathy. She was about to hit me with the heaviest one of a nesting set of glass ashtrays when the phone rang. I grabbed it and answered it and for some reason. It was Phyllis. She said that a group of people had showed up at their place, did we want to come up and join in? I relayed the message and Cathy said, "sure, that will be fun." Her anger was gone, and I lived to see another day.

One of the other events DOB held was the annual holiday cocktail party where we invited and celebrated men who were supportive of the organization, Sons of Bilitis or SOBs, like John and Philip Burton, among others. The SOBs did so much for us and we loved them all dearly.

These men, plus the fact that many of our members were prominent business women, helped me understand that I was not a pervert or mentally ill, but rather just a normal person attracted to women. I had always wanted kids, but had always listened to the opinion that gay people should not raise children. When I voiced this at one rap session, Phyllis Lyon said, "Good grief, Suzie, look around you, not one of these people was raised in a gay home. Del's daughter is a boy-crazy teenager, and there is no sign of gay there." About that same time Dubbi and I had become more than friends. I very much wanted to leave Cathy and the abuse that invariably occurred.

Milestone 33

Finally, one day while Cathy was at work, with Marti's help, I gathered all my belongings and moved into Dubbi's apartment. I left Cathy a note. At 11 when she came home, she started phoning us, at first she begged, then threatened, then demanded I come home. She kept it up all night. Finally, in the morning she said, "if you won't come home, I am coming after you."

Dubbi lived on the second floor and said, "she won't be able to get in the front door."

Just then, we heard glass shatter. One of us called the police, I don't remember who. The next thing we heard was her hammering on Dubbi's door. Dubbi said, "Open it! If she damages it, I will have to pay for it."

In rushed Cathy with a 30/30 rifle pointed at my belly. We wrestled across the floor, while I yelled for Dubbi to get something heavy and hit Cathy in the head. She said that she couldn't do that and she couldn't see her head to hit it. We wrestled with the rifle Cathy, trying to push it against me and me trying to push it away. It felt like we wrestled for hours. In reality, it was probably only a few minutes before we heard more hammering at the door and the words, "police!"

I yelled, "Open the door!"

Dubbi, totally disoriented, went the opposite way to the windows.

I yelled, "Not that way. The other way!"

She crossed back and went to open the door for the police. Two big, burly cops rushed in, came across the room, and grabbed the rifle.

One of them, bellowed, "What's going on?"

Cathy said, "We are lesbians, and she is trying to leave me."

The same officer said, "What do you want her to do lady? Get a divorce?!" I laughed.

To me he said to the other officer, "Oh, I like this one, cuff that one," indicating Cathy.

After the police lead her away, Dubbi and I sat in shock trembling. Eventually, one of us called Del and Phil and told them what had happened. They came immediately, got us and took us to breakfast at Miss Brown's restaurant on Clement St. It was decided that it would not be safe for us to stay in Dubbi's apartment and somehow they moved us into their place. Dell and Phil had a 24/7 open door policy for any Lesbian who needed a place. They also had a five-gallon water bottle by the door, three quarters full of pennies.

Their policy was that anyone was welcome to any of the pennies that needed them. Their two cats lived there as well: crazy Padashaw, and sweet Ace, who was so mellow everyone loved him. On the other hand, Padashaw would attack your legs around the bannister as you went up the stairs in their two-level home. Even though I had two part-time jobs at the time, one, at the Women's City club and the other at the YWCA, I didn't make much money. Phyllis got me a job in her office and Dell loaned me appropriate clothes. They were the most generous thoughtful and fun couple I have ever known.

After a few weeks, I managed to find a place with Dubbi and a view of the city. I really loved it. Obviously the view didn't mean a lot to Dubbi, since she was totally blind. I learned, at the risk of getting yelled at, to always put things back in the same place. I learned how to use your finger and fingernail to guide a key into a keyhole so you could unlock a door. And I learned to organize closets by articles and color, and also tricks for cooking and organization of life. I learned to read and write braille, so Dubbi and I could leave each other notes.

Years later, when my vision got worse and worse – I found it to be a minor inconvenience and not a really big deal. That along with all the aids and Blind school training the Marine Corps gave me makes it hardly noticeable. I felt I should keep Dubbi with me at all times, since she could not see. I had an assistant at the YWCA, Inga, who had an obvious crush on me. She was a sweet first-generation Norwegian-American who had just come back after spending a year in Norway. Dubbi, who had cooled on our relationship after the rifle incident, immediately got a crush on Inga.

The three of us, plus another guard from the YWCA started hanging out together all the time. Jo was an ex-school teacher who had lost her license when a teenager accused her of molesting her. I took her to see Del and Phil and they suggested that she talk to the psychologist who was a member of our organization. I don't know the details, but soon Jo was exonerated, she got her license back and accepted a job teaching at a junior college. She went to a teacher's conference and brought a girlfriend back with her just before school started. So now it was back to the three of us me, Dubbi and Inga. Dubbi kept insisting that she and I were not in a relationship. However, that didn't seem to hold water at night, as we frequently made love. This went on until the evening that I came home to find a totally empty apartment.

Milestone 35

She had taken all the furniture that we had gotten together except for two small pieces that were originally mine. A small table and a bookcase alone are not very conducive to facilitating a pleasant evening. She left a note saying that although she loved me as a friend, she did not want to live there anymore. She did not feel she could talk to me about it because she thought I would talk her into staying. She apologized for taking all the furniture and said that she would send me her new address and phone number soon.

I was sitting on the floor cross-legged, feeling sorry for myself when Inga showed up. She worked for Thomas Thomaear the caterer, and had often brought left over goodies and champagne. That evening she had two trays of goodies and two cold bottles of champagne. She was as shocked as I was about Dubbi's move. She sat and commiserated with me over the goodies she'd brought. Considering my mood, her crush, and the alcohol the inevitable happened. I had camping gear and so I pulled out two air mattresses and a couple of sleeping bags for us. It was a long way from comfortable but I was too out of it to care.

The next morning, I took her to breakfast at Miz Browns' and then we visited a mattress store on Market Street. I remember that we got a double bed innerspring for $40, which I felt was too much. Inga went to her family home and picked up a couple of chairs and a table that was in their garage. It seemed only right, knowing that she had been a virgin, that I invite her to move in.

It took a couple of months until school was out and then she moved in with me. I tried my best to be a considerate and loving partner and she seemed to be happy. Our relationship lasted eight years. She was sweet, kind, and very intelligent. As soon as she graduated college, she got a teaching job close to my apartment which she said was her main excuse for moving in with me. Her parents were very cordial to me although it was clear that her father did not approve of the relationship. Her mother never seemed to notice and her two brothers less approved.

Book 3 – kids, kids, kids!

Milestone 36

While Inga was in school, Marty and I went to a bar called Kelly's on Steiner Street This woman named Adele who had come to San Francisco from New York only a month or so before, was teaching us a new dance that was sweeping the nation. The directions were: "While grinding out a cigarette with the toe of one foot, you pulled an imaginary towel back and forth behind you, as if drying your butt." It was a lot of fun and was called the twist.

I was a rotten dancer, but I loved it because I didn't have to match steps with anyone. Later that evening I found myself shooting pool with Adele. When we were ready to go, I said, I'll see you next Friday." She said she wouldn't be there next Friday, and when I asked why, she said that she was having an abortion.

When I asked her why, she said that she didn't want a baby, I said, "give it to me, I'd love to have a baby!" I told her that Phyllis Lyon had once called me a "latent heterosexual" because I wanted kids so much.

Adele said, well, I might do that, but you'd have to guarantee me five years because I don't care for small children.

I said, "You've got it." And our deal was thereby struck. This was the third woman I had made this offer to, and the only one who actually accepted it. Twice while reading tarot to young women who were regulars, I had made that same offer. I offered to let them stay with me, but they decided to have their babies after all.

Adele said she was having a boy and would name him Eric, and I said, "Better make it Erika, it's a girl." "She said, I always have boys."

I said, "not this time." We became good friends and nine months later little Erika entered the world. I'd been right. Inga and I were in The Ladder office, collating the latest issue when the phone call came. Three days later, I carried little Erika out of the hospital.

By this time, Inga and I had furniture, appliances, and a beautiful black cat named Butch. We put a crib in our bedroom, and we became a family. As it happened, I had been fired from my job at the women's city club. I refused to allow a club member, who was a harpist in the San Francisco Symphony Orchestra, into the pool.

She had been drinking and I felt she was too drunk to safely go in. I was told it was a social situation and therefore I was not allowed to deny any member the use of the pool. So I quit, as my boss fired me. As a result, I had time on my hands, which made it easy for me to take Erika. As it happened Adele turned out to be a very good mother. She frequently had Erika on weekends and overnight. Erika stayed with me this way until she was eight years old.

It all worked very well, we were happy and Erika was a darling little girl. I got my child care license. The last visit from the worker who vetted me for the license was interesting. She spent quite a long time beating around the bush, saying she had to ask me something and apologizing for it and made comments about me being a single woman. I saw it coming and so when she finally got around to it, and asked if I was a lesbian, with a perfectly straight face, I said, "no, I am Catholic."

She immediately accepted it and signed my license. I think she thought that I thought lesbian was a religion. Actually, perhaps it is. I was very devoted to it. Heh. Within a matter of days Phyllis called me and told me that there was a little baby boy that I needed to go get. She explained that a lesbian and a gay guy had gotten together and thought it would be fun to make a baby. They had already fallen out as friends by the time the baby was born. The mother, who we all knew was a bit alcoholic and a bit crazy, was not taking good care of him. They had spoken to her and by the time I arrived, she had him, his clothes, and furniture ready for me to take.

Erika was just learning to walk at this time, and she adored the baby, KP. The first two years of KP's life were frustrating for me. His blood mother, after weeks of ignoring him, would suddenly announce she was taking him for the weekend. This petrified him because naturally, he never spent enough time around her to know her. When he was 10 months old, she announced she was going back to Kentucky to visit family and taking him with her. I was so upset, that Adele gave me Valium to help me get through the six days he was gone.

It was even worse, when I heard, via the grapevine, that she was thinking of leaving him in Kentucky when she came back. At the time, KP's mother was living with a super-butch black woman known as Lucky. Lucky and I had become friends and so I immediately called Lucky and asked her for help. She said, "No prob, babe." Within an hour, she called back to report that they were both flying back the next day. His mother dropped KP off with me on the way home from the airport, obviously glad to be rid of him and he clung to me like a lifeline.

It turned out that he had brought back a form of virulent stomach flu that went through the household like lightening. Inga then infected half her students before she got sick and Adele wiped out her office. I think our household was responsible for infecting a large part of San Francisco. In spite of all this, I was overjoyed my boy was home. After that, things went along swimmingly until KP was about two. At that time, KP had an ear infection, which was not uncommon for him. We had just returned from the pediatrician when I got a call from his mom.

She informed me that her psychiatrist told her that she needed KP in order to get herself together and she was coming to get him. I begged her not to, he didn't even know her, had a bad ear infection, and was upset. She said she could give him his medicine as easy as I could and he would get over not knowing her after a while. So she came and got him. She told me that because she was working she had hired a babysitter to watch him in the apartment. I told her that he had a follow-up doctor's appointment on Monday. She said that she couldn't make it because she was working.

I told her that under the circumstances that I would come and get him and take him. When I went to get him, I noticed that the bottle of medicine was sitting beside his bed, totally full. The babysitter was an elderly woman who had been asleep in the other room while KP was in his bed crying. The woman told me the baby's mom told her that the medicine was not important, and that it was something that I had "thought up" and to forget it. When I got to the pediatrician he told me that KPs ears were much worse. He sympathized. Both the baby and I were in tears as I explained to the doctor what had happened. He said that he wished he could help me, and if I ended up in court, he would testify. He said that since he couldn't depend on KP getting the medicine, he would have to take other steps.

He gave the poor baby a shot in each thigh. We were both sobbing when we left the office and everyone there commiserated with us. I couldn't bring myself to take him back to that apartment and figured out a way to keep him around. About a year later we found that KP's mom had given birth to a baby girl and a friend asked whether I wanted her. I thought KP should have his little sister and said, "absolutely." Her name was Noel because she'd been born at Christmas time. She was a child of mixed blood. Then I heard she was dealing with a couple from Salt Lake City for Noel. When KP was seven he was tested and placed in the top three percent of the population. He quit high school at 16 and enrolled in junior college. He finally settled on computers as his life's work and has become a super geek. He was 19 when I adopted the other six kids, I think he has always resented them. He now tells us that he doesn't need us.

I think someday he will regret that—hopefully not too late. I love KP with all my heart, but I am not crazy about his attitude. But nine months after I adopted KP, I got a brother and sister. As it worked out, I got KP nine months after getting Erika; then Mike and Deena, nine months after getting KP. It was as if the Universe had taken a hand. Mikey was 3, and Deena was a year old. When I went to get them, she wore a diaper that probably had not been changed in 12 hours and a bottle full of clabbered milk.

She was very fat and made only one sound—da. Her hair was thin and didn't grow down the sides. Mikey's head was shaved and he only said, "Wa is it?" and "No." I was only supposed to keep them during the day, but their young, spacey mother asked if I could keep them over night because she had an important job interview. I said yes even though it was not convenient because my mother was visiting at that time.

The next day, late in the afternoon, I got a phone call. It was their mother. She said she had been in an automobile accident and was in St. John's hospital in Vallejo and would be there four or five days. She asked if I would please keep the kids. And, of course, I told her, yes. I immediately called information and asked for St John's hospital in Vallejo. As I suspected there was no such hospital, nor any hospital that sounded remotely similar. Adele had faithfully paid me $85 per month and had never failed. KPs mother had given me one check that had bounced and never offered another. With two more mouths to feed and diapers to buy, that meant I would need more money.

Thanks to social services, I had to fill out an information sheet when I took on new kids and I had the kids' father's phone number. I called him immediately and he said he would be right over. He explained that they were separated, and that while he had not seen it, neighbors had told him that she had been drinking heavily. He said that Mikey, while playing in the backyard a few months before had been called to lunch. His mother had set the food out for him and then decided to take a bath. She fell asleep in the tub, and when she got out, she noticed that Mikey wasn't where she'd left him and hadn't touched his food. She searched for him, and after an hour, called the police for help. When he was finally found, they figured out that he had climbed to the roof (four stories high) and had fallen three stories down to the flat top of the garage.

He was in a coma for several weeks and they didn't know what to expect over the next few years. Their father worked nights and asked me to watch the kids during the week until he could find a housekeeper. He never did hire that housekeeper, but instead picked them up on Saturday and dropped them off on Monday. As they grew, Mikey got better and better, although he always was somewhat slow, Deena turned into a little fireball and Erika's best friend. I was very protective of the children, constantly keeping them surrounded with love, light, and positive thinking. One time, Mikey came in crying saying that the neighbor kid had stepped on a wooly worm and killed it. Erika and Deena immediately started crying too. KP was too young to understand, but he joined in too, I guess to keep them company.

I realized that the kids were too sensitive and I was too protective and they would not be ready to meet the world if I kept them surrounded by cotton batting. They were super sensitive to the world around them and as well as to each other. Once while Mikey was at kindergarten the girls came running inside saying he'd fallen and hurt his knee badly. I reminded them that he was at school. At that time the phone rang. It was the principal telling me to come and get him. He had a badly lacerated knee which required stitches and probably staying off it as much as possible for a few days.

I spent a great deal of time taking the kids camping, to the park, and to the zoo, etc. One time when we returned from camping, each one helped unload the car, carrying what they could. Deena, being three, carried the lightest load. I gave her a flat, folded air mattress to carry into the house. When she reached the porch she dropped it and a little yellow scorpion popped out. I was right behind her and so I quickly stepped over and squashed it.

As a rule, I never killed small creatures without need. Though we were in Napa County we had camped next to some folks from Mexico. I was afraid; it could have been one of the deadly ones from Mexico and I didn't want to take a chance. Over the years, various children came and went. I had had a number of charges like Kay and her sisters, Dawn and Robin, a (different) Mikey with a 17-second attention span, a beautiful three-year old, Theresa, with hair down to her rear. She and KP became engaged at aged three. (Theresa, you should have made it happen because KP is now a rich computer maven in Portland). Theresa's father was a Hells Angels who often brought her on his bike.

When he came to get her, he put her and KP on the seat in front of him and rode them around the block. He was very generous and brought me a lid of Acapulco Gold or "Panama Red. I swear that was absolutely different stuff than what people currently smoke. I tried this new stuff not long ago, for old time's sake, with a pot smoking friend, and afterwards, I was sick for three days.

Milestone 37

I'd been taking classes at the metaphysical center in San Francisco. They invited me to read astrology for $10 per reading, which consisted of a horoscope and an explanation of same. Through no one's fault, Inga and I had come to an equitable parting of ways. I now needed additional income, so I started doing readings twice a week. Inga moved a block and a half away and took the kids on some weekends. At the same time, I was taking a Tarot class with Maggie Anthony. So when the Metaphysical center decided to have a read in (a weekend featuring dozens of practitioners of the psychic arts) I was invited to try my hand at it.

Even though many of the people there were well known, I became the most requested Tarot reader at the event and read over 35 people that weekend. Because of this, the manager of the Metaphysical center invited me to read Tarot two additional evenings a week at the center. Maggie lived in Berkley and had two little kids and was glad to cut her trips to once a week. I actually read two to three nights a week for roughly 13 years and became quite well known in San Francisco. I was even quoted in Herb Cain's column and was invited to speak in various high school and college classes.

I don't know if other readers are affected this way, but I don't remember a reading ten minutes after finishing it. I never recognize a client until they had come to me for a reading several times, which made for some funny situations. On one occasion, a small Asian man walked into my office at the metaphysical center and said, "here is your baby." I stared at him speechless as he handed me a baby that looked about four month old. He kept saying, "It's your baby." After he repeated this a third time, a young woman came bustling into the room. She stared at the look on my face and laughed. She said, "You don't remember, do you?"

I confessed that I did not. She explained that a year earlier, just before she left for the Peace Corp, I had told her she would have a baby. She told me that it was impossible. Then she had met Van (the young Asian man) and Viola! Here was the baby. They asked me to bless the child and knowing that I was a Pagan, asked me to call on my goddess to protect him. I only remember readings if something important brings them to mind. Two other readings that come to mind were with young women who were considering abortion. I dealt with it as I had with Ericka's mother, offering to take the child or offering to let them stay with me during their pregnancy. They both decided to have the babies. One of them married her rather wealthy young man (I don't know the outcome of that one).

The other baby (a girl) grew up to be a very successful attorney in Berkley, CA.

The funniest one I remember occurred when a young woman and her mother came to have readings together. As I read for the girl, the mother kept saying things like, "that's not true or that doesn't fit." The girl said, "you are wrong mother, you just don't know. It actually fits perfectly."

When I read for the mother, I told her that she would find and marry a doctor. She said that she didn't move in those circles. Because of her attitude, I refused to accept her money. I encountered her again on a Halloween read-in in the basement of Akron on the wharf in San Francisco.

As I read, I noticed a woman standing at the barrier waving and calling to me. She was standing with a short balding man in his fifties and they were both grinning like Cheshire cats. Eventually, I went over to them.

She explained, "this is my doctor, my podiatrist, isn't he wonderful." She handed me a fifty-dollar bill as payment for my services and as an apology. They invited me to their wedding. I read for many celebrities, Marge Champion (the famous dancer), Agnes Morehead, and others, and many of the cast members of the various plays on Gary St, like "Jesus Christ Superstar."

Probably one of the most life altering readings happened in my home in Concord. One day I got a call from a young man saying that he was returning my call. He said that he had been told to call me by a note he found on his desk. He said his name was Jack Steen and he was a social worker in Contra Costa County.

When I didn't recognize him, puzzled, he asked, "Why would someone tell me to call you?"

I said I didn't know unless he was looking for an astrologer or Tarot reader. He said he wasn't looking, but he'd love to have his Tarot read. I explained that I read in San Francisco and didn't much want to bring it into my home as I had small children. He begged and pleaded a little and I decided that a social worker would be okay and I agreed he could come. He started to talk about himself but I asked him not to until after the reading, please. He came the next day at lunch time and I discovered that he was one of the sweetest, nicest gay men. He was from Kokomo Indiana, 18 miles north of Indianapolis. I was from Franklin, 18 miles south of Indianapolis. He had two lovers who ran The Swan antique store on Market Street. They had been a threesome for years.

He had a sister in Indiana that he wanted me to read for. He said Cindy was gay, but had never admitted it. She had two daughters, was divorced and was quite unhappy with her life. He wanted me to read for her and tell her that she was gay. I told him that I couldn't do that, I could only point out any tendencies or indications, but in the long run, it was up to her. As it happened, fate stepped in and by the time she came out she brought her lover Carolyn with her. We became bosom friends (Carolyn, Cindy, and I). Maggie Anthony and I became very good friends and spent a lot of time together. I learned a lot from her. But once again Marty took a hand in my life. Mikey and Deena now had moved to Washington with their Dad. Marty introduced me to a friend of a friend who had a three-year-old girl, little Kay, who was epileptic.

Because she had to work, her mother Bea, had to place her in a nursery school. The teacher was so frightened of the idea of a seizure that she carried Kay around on her hip all day. I had shared a room with an epileptic in the naval Hospital. I had learned that if you talk to someone having a seizure, they will attempt to respond to your directions. Bea asked if I would take Kay and I said absolutely no problem. She was a beautiful mixed race child. Bea was Caucasian, and Bea's Daddy was African- American. They were a totally hippie couple and one of the first things he did was to offer me a hit off a joint. It was 1966 and I also was caring for a baby girl named Mary and Mikey, six, with the 17-second attention span.

My routine was that when the parents came to my house to get their kids, we all sat at the table, discussed the day and the kids while having a glass of wine and sharing a joint. Because I had KP and Erika, I didn't get out at night any longer; weekend evenings were usually spent with friends, talking, smoking a joint and listening to The White Album. Typically, we got the munchies so bad we would eat everything in sight, and we laughed so hard it hurt. The next day, I could never remember what had been so funny.

Milestone 38

In 1968, all one heard about was LSD. It was legal and psychiatrists were handing it out like popcorn. One didn't take it like a drug, but rather one had a guide and went on a trip. By this time, I had become involved with a woman who was into pot and other forms of drugs. She talked me into doing LSD one evening with a couple of friends as guides. The pill had a Swiss government imprint and came straight from a psychiatrist's office, so we knew it was pure. They gave me the pill and then we drove to Golden Gate Park. They thought it would be a nice place to be when the hallucinations started. We were standing by the duck pond when I noticed the waves were rounded and seemed to be dancing. The ducks were asleep in a group on the other side of the pond. I remember telling my guide that I was going to walk across the pond and pet them.

She said, "I'm sure you could, but you know what they do to people who walk on water? I think we had better go home."

They lived in an apartment over a store on Valencia Street in San Francisco. When we arrived, they presented me with a bouquet of beautiful golden zinnias. As I was talking about how lovely they were, I noticed that huge drops of blood were oozing out of the tops of them. I was horrified that they had been cut from their roots just to give to me. It was years before I could stand having cut flowers around me.

The many growing potted plants in the home were different entirely. The leaves of each plant became a different crystalline color and danced. Lori fed me homemade yogurt and I saw a thick white waterfall imprinted with Egyptian symbols flowing over everything. I mentioned needing to go to the ladies' room and my guide warned me not to look in the mirror. If I did, she said I would frighten myself. Of course I looked in the mirror—no way I couldn't. When I did, I saw an animal that looked half wolf and half gorilla staring at me. I thought this was hilarious and laughed aloud. My guide asked what I saw and why it didn't frighten me.

I asked her why I would be frightened of a hallucination? "After all", I quipped, "I know I took acid and I know what is going on."

Then I told her that I was going to the room at the end of the hall. Her partner's ex had left a room full of huge oil paintings and I wanted to see how they would look. My guide said that I couldn't go there alone, and I said, "Excuse me?! I am 34. I can do anything I want!" There was a lovely armchair in the middle of the room and I sat there to look at a painting of a child on a merry-go-round. It began to get very dark. I looked down to see a rat gnawing at something close to my foot. Within minutes the room was festooned with dark dust-filled cobwebs.

The child on the merry-go-round became a wolf snapping at a pony. There were huge spiders in the webs, in the windows and in the fireplace. I got up and ran back to my guide. This time Lori was the one who laughed. "I told you that you couldn't do it," she said.

"We will see about that," I said, and drank a little of the wine she gave me. At least I think it was wine and then I started back down the hall. I came to a spot that I can only call an impenetrable force field. It stopped me dead. It took about three tries, but I finally got through and made it to the room. It still would have been a goth's delight and I sat down and started taking control of the hallucination. I told my mind that it was full of love and light. I demanded that it ignore the shadows and see through to the truth.

Slowly at first and then with a bang, everything turned from back to bright and clean. The boy on the merry-go-round was going up and down, waving and throwing me kisses. In the other paintings people were dancing, riding horses and generally in a happy mood. My guide asked, "how in the hell did you do it?"

I replied, "By demanding the truth." Since I now suffer from COPD (Crappy Old People's Disease) I realized this is another blessing. Sort of like having lived with a blind person prepared me for my low vision, the acid trip prepared me for things to come.

Milestone 39

It was about this time when my friend Maggie Anthony invited David St. Clair to lecture at the Metaphysical center where I read Tarot. His topic, "The Religions of Brazil." Erika was spending the night with Adele, so I took KP with me. He was now 3 years old and a great traveling companion. If he got tired, he'd just curl up on my lap and go to sleep. David spoke about going to a three-week assignment and it taking three more years for him to get away and come back. He spoke about the goddess Yemanja, the other gods and goddesses in Brazil and some spells he had encountered. When the seminar was over, everyone was chatting and having coffee.

KP woke up and said, "I want to see the lady with David."

I said, "You mean Maggie?"

He said, "No, I know Maggie. I mean the black lady in the blue dress that is floating behind David, and isn't got no feet."

I took him over and told David, chuckling, and David went ghost-white. "Oh no," he said. "They told me she would follow me, that's Yemanja."

I didn't put much stock in it until later that week when I had a dream. I dreamed I did a spell and then had to laugh, because I'd never been into that sort of thing. A few days later, David invited me to dinner, as he wanted to interview me for the book he was writing, "The Psychic World of California."

Over dinner, chuckling, I told him about the spell in the dream only to see him turn dead pale. "That is one of the most closely guarded spells in the Macumba religion. It is extremely dangerous and can cause all kinds of havoc and misery. Please never tell anyone." Then he said, "Yemanja has chosen you. Better pay attention."

I have never used this spell, told anyone, or been tempted to since it fits the definition of "black magic" by interfering with someone's free will. He explained that Yemanja, the goddess of the sea and the mother of us all, liked feminine things like flowers, perfume and jewelry as offerings, etc. It wasn't long before I had an occasion to test the situation.

Since Inga had moved, I had no car and with a house full of little kids, I really needed one. During this particular time, a white witch was giving classes at the Metaphysical center. I decided to employ one of the techniques she was teaching. It was said to create a space for what you wanted, taking the expression: "Nature abhors a vacuum", literally.

I placed two sawhorses in front of my house about a car's length apart, and stretched a piece of crepe paper between them. When people asked what it was for, I said, "For my car." When they asked what car, I explained it was the one that the goddess was going to send me. In less than a week, having told three to four groups of people this, the young couple who had served as my guides for my acid trip, looked at each other and said, "Tarzan" in unison, and then, "We will be right back."

Before long, looking out of the window I saw him moving the saw horses and then parking a battered-looking Chevy Bel Aire in the same space. She parked another car behind him, and then they came into the house grinning like Cheshire cats.

He handed me a set of keys and the title paper and said, "There is your car".

I couldn't believe my eyes, and as much as I wanted it to happen, I was still surprised when it did. It was pretty beat up. There was a hole in the floorboard in the back, that had to be covered up with a board and one of the windows would not roll up all the way. I got a foam-rubber bolster and covered it with Naugahyde. I acquired three webbing belts at the army surplus store. After securing the bolster to the frame I also attached three web belts. I had one of the car seats that went over the front seat back. KP rode in the baby seat next to me, but the older kids were secured in the back seat.

Once I had the car all fixed up, I copied the title, collected a couple of bottles of perfume, a candle and some flowers, strapped the kids in and we headed for the beach at the first low tide. It was one of those rare warm and beautiful days at San Francisco Ocean Beach. While the kids paddled around collecting shells and pretty rocks I went as close to the edge of the water as possible. I dug a pit deep enough to protect the candle from the wind and deposited all the items in it. I sat on the sand, watching the kids, as the ocean slowly moved up to take my offerings. Tarzan now belonged to Yemanja. I never had a flat tire, car trouble or a ticket during the three years I drove it. It was in Tarzan I first learned about reincarnation. I'd never given it much thought.

Once when driving along, KP, sitting in the baby's seat, leaned over to ask me something. He said, "When I die, will those same two guys help me get to my new body? I think I have forgotten how I did it."

That shook me up. Another time, he said, "Who was my mommy before you were my mommy?"

It freaked me out and I mumbled, "I don't know. "

He leaned over and patted me and said, "Its okay, Mommy, you've always been my Mommy, sooner or later, and you always will be. That's our agreement, don't you remember?"

He gave me? a whole new outlook on life and I started some serious reading.

Not long after that, KP displayed a hidden talent for dealing with animals. It was a warm sunny afternoon and KP was playing alone in the backyard. I went to get him and told him it was time to take a little rest. He asked if his friend could come with him.

I asked, "What friend?" He pointed to something next to the swing set. I moved a little closer and saw a large, orange dragonfly following and swooping in time with the swing. I said, "well he probably won't want to come inside, but he can wait for you."

He took my hand and we walked across the yard and up the steps. The weird thing was, the dragonfly came along with us, just above his shoulder all the way to the door. As we walked inside, it zipped away across the yard and I assumed that was the last time that we would ever see it. KP took a two-hour nap, and after some juice and cookies headed back outside.

He was not all the way down the steps before I heard him say, "Here's Buggy."

I looked out and saw a big orange dragonfly following him toward the swing set. These dragonfly appearances lasted for about three days until Buggy finally disappeared. KP explained that Buggy had gone to visit his family and didn't seem to be too upset.

Later that summer I took Erika and KP to Indiana to visit my parents. They still lived on their small farm with a few sheep and pigs just two miles outside the county seat. There was a fenced pasture along one side of my parent's property and the children had been there watching the sheep and feeding them grass. I was sitting on the porch swing talking to my mother when Erika came running up. She said "KP is petting a funny looking kitty."

Since I knew my mother did not keep pets, I was immediately on my feet. KP was squatted down in front of a little black critter with a white stripe down it's back. I said, "Oh no." I knew that at any second he would be sprayed unmercifully. I told Erika to stay with me and started calling him as gently as I could. I told him to walk slowly away and come to me. He said, "No mommy! Kitty." as he was gently petting the little skunk on its head and back.

After about five minutes of this, he finally decided to come to me. The sweet little creature wandered away across the pasture and my only slightly smelly son came to join us. He had not been sprayed, only picked up a bit of odor from the proximity and a quick bath took care of that.

Milestone 40

Two years after that, Erika was playing with the Maidu boy who lived two doors down. It was a big family, and the kids were great, but the father was a heroin addict. I was seeing a chiropractor at the time, and on about the third visit he told me that my liver was enlarged and I should go see my doctor. I was really feeling bad, so I talked Inga into taking me to my doctor downtown. He told me I had Hepatitis and should check into the general hospital. I was sitting in the waiting room of the hospital when the female doctor came out. She yelled "who's the woman who thinks she has Hepatitis?"

When I stood up, she looked at me and said, "Oh My God, you really have hepatitis." I guess I must have been bright yellow by that time. She looked me up and down and said that I wouldn't like the Hepatitis ward because it is full of loud crazy hippies. She told me, go home, go to bed and make sure you eat three solid meals a day; we can't do much more than that for you.

Inga said, don't worry, I will take care of her and make sure she eats right. It was really good of her under the circumstances. I was told by the doctor to go to a certain lab and have blood drawn every few days. The first time I was at the lab, I fainted and the laboratory tech refused to see me again, and so the doctor started coming to my house. Doctors did that then, it was wonderful.

As a result of our neighborhood heroin addict, Erika, and both of the parents of baby Mary (one of my charges) all landed in the hospital with Hepatitis. About this time, my cousin Paul showed up with three guys, a girl, and a pet boa. They took an apartment and started looking for a gig as a couple of them were musicians and the third one wanted to be.

Paul took a job as a bartender in one of the local gay bars. He was totally straight, but he let them think what they wanted, and since he was very good looking and well built, he made lots of tips. We had an old guitar that the kids messed with and one of his friends asked if he could have it. He took it home, restrung it and painted hippie symbols on it. He taught himself to play and within a month was the featured member of the band.

They were fantastic. They got an offer of a gig in LA and so the band left Paul and his girlfriend in San Francisco. He was in and out of the house a lot and I loved having a family member close. That Thanksgiving I had 25 people for dinner in my tiny two-bedroom house. Paul and his girl, some Tarot clients, gays with no place to go, and parents of the kids I watched. It was great fun.

Milestone 41

Shortly after that I was in the hospital. A routine Pap smear had turned up bad. As a result, I had a D&C and then 50 hours radiation, followed by a hysterectomy. The Doctor told me that the hysterectomy probably was not needed, but since Ronald Reagan was cutting things out of the budget, he was afraid that I would not be able to get it when I needed it. It became obvious after the hysterectomy that I was not up to taking care of the kids again. So my babies were scattered to the four winds except for KP whom I had adopted, and little Danny whom I had had full time for three years.

Adele took Erika to live with her full time. Fortunately, I had a couple of friends in Berkley who were moving to Boston. The apartment that they vacated had been handed down from friend to friend for years and so there was no deposit and the rent had remained quite low (in my turn, when I left, I passed it down to Kay's mother). Once again, my goddess had come through, and even brought me a moving posse' in the form of my Hells Angels friend and all his buddies... the only charge was a case of beer.

Milestone 42

By this time, Erika was eight and living with Adele. As a result, we had an extra bedroom. Marti introduced me to a friend who needed a place right then. Due to a bad break up, she had lost most of her things including her car. At the same time, a friend had offered me a much newer Ford Fairlane, also free, so I offered her Tarzan. I explained to her that the car belonged to Yemanja and that she should go to the ocean and thank Yemanja for the loan. I offered to take her to the beach with me when I went to give Yemanja the title to the Ford. She smirked and said sarcastically, "Oh yeah, I am really going to do that."

Less than two weeks later, the motor blew and Tarzan was gone. A few weeks later, Dee moved a friend in with her. She was a sweet young woman who had left a bad relationship, and as a result, had no income. She asked if she could stay for free for a couple of weeks, until she got a job. At the time, Dee and I were taking turns buying groceries, and the young woman was watching KP when I was at the Metaphysical center.

It seemed fine until I came home and was told that KP and I were not welcome to join them at the table. She said that we would have to buy our own groceries from then on, even though she owed me quite a bit already. I took KP and drove to my friend Judy Mars' house. Judy was my co-reader at the Metaphysical center and the most psychic human being I knew.

After she fed us, and commiserated with us, she told me to go back, and tell Dee to leave. KP was seven and felt in some way responsible. Dee had complained about him watching Saturday morning cartoons, saying it disturbed them and he felt bad. By the time we got back, I was so angry, I was afraid to talk to her and so I wrote her a note. I told her to be out by the weekend, and to take her girlfriend and her four cats, or I wouldn't be responsible for my behavior.

This was a Thursday. And by Saturday morning she was gone, lock stock, and kitty cat. This was just before Christmas and it was a very lean time for me. I was only able to get KP a Donny Osmond record and a toy car for Christmas. A good friend gave him a huge ride-on fire engine and my mother sent him a huge box full of goodies. I used what little money I had left to take him to his favorite hamburger joint, where they specialized in 23 different types. My mother sent me a huge round of FIGI cheese; I lived on that for the rest of the month, giving all the food in the house to KP.

Milestone 43

Judy had told me that the question of what would happen was already answered and I should not worry. Sure enough, right at the first of the year, one of the young women I had read cards for invited me to dinner. She was a 25-year-old lesbian, Diane, with a three-year-old son, Che'. I was 42, with a 7 year old son. Within 2 weeks, she had moved in with me.

She worked at an insurance company and made quite good money. She loved good food and insisted on plenty of it. That was a two edged sword. The availability was wonderful, but I started gaining weight. By this time, I was taking care of her son while she was at work. My good friend Leslie, who was living in Berkley, was taking care of KP, Danny, and Che' while I was doing readings. Diane another very bright woman. She was Jewish, born in Brooklyn New York to a borderline kosher family. She graduated from a performing arts high school at 16 and spent a year in Israel on a kibbutz. She was very much involved in the human rights movement and had been one of the riders on the bus that went to Arkansas to support the young black people entering integrated schools for the first time.

When she came back from Israel she became involved with a young black man from the Caribbean who had been a chef on the Matson Line cruise ships. This is where she got her inclination for very rich, expensive foods. They had opened a restaurant in New York, but it had gone bust due to his mismanagement. That is when they moved to San Francisco. They both became involved in drugs. One time, Diane took something that would not let her come down. In desperation, she turned to the diggers, who were a group in San Francisco who would help people on drugs.

They assigned a rather good looking young man, currently awaiting incarceration on drug charges to spend time with her until she came down. Apparently that took about 12 hours and you might imagine what could have transpired during the time. Even though Che's birth certificate lists his father as being black, he was a blonde, blue eyed baby boy. Diane chose to never tell the real father of her son about his paternity. She instead chose to glamorize the black man to Che'. She neglected to tell her son that he had dumped her because she refused to prostitute herself to get them money. Diane and I were together eight years and it was not unlike living on a roller coaster.

She was bright, witty, and informed. She frequently beat me at scrabble or gin rummy. One of her endearing and annoying habits was to become obsessed with fads. The first one was country music. The station on my car radio was called the blaze and it played all kinds of country music. She made fun of it a couple of times, but when I offered to change the station, she protested, no, no! She finally admitted that she liked it, but because her family had made fun of it, she had followed suit.

After that we were required to buy cowboy shirts, boots, and belts with big buckles. We attended every country concert that came to the area and she particularly liked Donna Fargo and her song "Superman." From the beginning, Diane really did not like the apartment in Berkley and wanted us to get a house. This started a travel Odyssey that landed us in Concord CA four years later.

The first move was to Albany, to a house next door to the landlord's family. Living next to the landlord's family is never a good idea. His wife was quite nosey and very interested in our living arrangements. The landlord himself was a little league coach and was very adamant that our boys get involved. I found his ten-year-old son in bed with KP one afternoon when I went to get KP to go shopping.

I made no comment, just said, come on, we need to leave, he said that the kid wanted to play something called "honeymoon" but he didn't like it much. I told him that I preferred that he didn't do that, and he said he didn't really want to anyway. Despite having a lesbian mother and being around them all his young life, JP grew up to be straight as a string. He is a shining example of the fact that gays are born, not made. The icing on the cake was when the twelve-year old daughter while babysitting four-year-old Che' asked him to touch her private parts. Little Che' thought it was funny and told us, thinking it was a joke. We moved the next month.

Milestone 44

The next move was to San Leandro, into a very nice townhouse complex with a swimming pool. Diane had placed little Che' in the Jewish kindergarten in the Temple in Oakland. KP walked to school and there was a teenaged girl next door who babysat without the hanky-panky. It was lovely and convenient and we would have stayed there until Erika's stepfather brought her to visit. At this time, her mother had gone into a drug treatment program, and Erika had been placed with a Japanese family in the area who had a daughter her age. It turned out that the father had been molesting his daughter all along. When the mother and daughter were away for the weekend, he attempted to molest Erika.

She had bitten and scratched the man so badly that he had to tell his wife that he had fallen in a rosebush, and had threatened Erika to keep her mouth shut or else. She did not want to tell her stepfather and had begged to come to me. I sent him to get Erika's things immediately and told him to turn the bastard in to the police. He never did. He claimed the guy had cried and begged and said that he would never do it again. I think he got paid off. Years later, the mother and daughter came to Erika and asked why she had left so abruptly, it turned out that he had continued to molest his daughter until her late teens, when she finally fought back.

Milestone 45

Our next move was to Castro Valley, brought about by another white magic spell. First of all, we asked the powers that be to look kindly on our needs. I asked for a comfortable three-bedroom home. Diane asked for a convenient bus line to San Francisco. Erika asked for a dishwasher. KP asked for bunkbeds and Che' asked for a goldfish pond—we all laughed. The next day, I picked up a throwaway newspaper from the back yard. I opened it for kicks and in the wanted section was one notice for rent: a three-bedroom home in Castro Valley. It was being rented fully furnished for two years by a family going to Saudi Arabia to work. It was beautiful. It had a canopy bed in the girl's room, bunks in the boy's room, a dishwasher in the kitchen, bus to the BART one block away and wonder of wonders, a goldfish pond.

A huge garage was built underneath it. My cousin Paul showed up with his van and girlfriend and they moved in there. Unfortunately, it only lasted a year because the family hated Saudi Arabia and asked for their house back. Next stop, Concord, CA. We found a nice little three-bedroom home one block from the park. The park had a train which ran around a little lake and a miniature Ferris wheel. On weekends and summer afternoons you could buy sodas, snow cones and cotton candy. A block and a half in the other direction was a neighborhood swimming pool that belonged to the residents of that area. Also close by was a shopping center, a grammar school and a junior high school. It was absolutely the perfect place to raise kids. Erika became involved in tennis, KP in Boy Scouts and Che' in little league.

Milestone 46

Life could have been idyllic, except Diane had a violent streak that kept escalating. She had always been given to occasional unreasonable rages aimed at Che' or me, I always interceded for Che' and never allowed her to hit him. We were in Concord the first time she actually struck me. She always apologized profusely afterwards and usually took us all out to dinner. I noticed a pattern and thought perhaps she had a form of epilepsy because she had an aunt that was so afflicted. I convinced her to see a doctor, and since we knew no one, we went to see the doctor that serviced the little league kids.

The man was an idiot; he diagnosed her as schizophrenic and gave her meds that turned her into a zombie. I knew he was wrong and put a stop to the pills right away. She was one of the highest ranking clerical workers in one of the most prestigious law firms in San Francisco. She was one of the first of their employees to use a computer in the office and was pulling down a fantastic salary. The pattern continued and the violence accelerated. The last straw occurred when her friend Linda took us to a Grateful Dead concert. I thought it was nice enough, but all their music sounded alike. Diane, however, dove in headfirst and became a total "Deadhead." She filled the house with their music, bought tee-shirts and attended all their concerts that were within driving range.

She often went early to the concert location—as much as 24 hours in advance—to camp out and party with other Deadheads. She'd leave Che' with me. I felt sorry for the kid. I know he felt abandoned. I did the best I could with him. Probably because of the age difference, Che' never quite bonded with KP or Erika. As time went on, the rages continued until Erika became totally fed up and moved in with Adele, who had bought a mobile home a few miles away. By now, KP was 15 and Che' was 11. Diane and I were hardly talking, and I decided to bring things to a head. When I told Diane that I would not be able to watch Che' that weekend because I was going away, she exploded. When I picked up the phone and said I was going to call a friend, she stabbed my arm and hand five times with a ball point pen. What was it with lesbians wanting to kill me rather than let me leave?! I'm certainly no prize petunia, just an average nice person, at least I try to be.

A ball point pen may not seem like a deadly weapon, but it went all the way to the bone and blood poured down my arm. I managed to get to my car and lock the door with her hot on my heels. She kicked the car, hammered the window and finally ripped the antennae right off. As I drove away, she chased me halfway down the street screaming invectives while the neighbors listened, it was so embarrassing. I went to the emergency room. They cleaned me up, put a stitch in each hole and gave me a tetanus shot. They wanted me to talk to a policeman, but I left before he got there, I didn't want Diane to get in trouble. I located KP and told him not to go home and went to a friend's house. At that point, I called her and told her that I was not talking to the police, but I wanted her out ASAP.

Three days later she called me and told me that she had moved out. KP and I returned to the house. After Diane and Che' moved out, I had to supplement my income from Tarot readings and went into Real Estate. After about a year, I was selling a huge four bedroom home across from the high school. We were doing a great deal of creative financing at the time and I was able to buy the house myself using my commission as the down payment. Like many, I had a balloon payment at the end of the year and the house payments were $1000 a month, which kept me jumping. I applied for some foster kids and even had a girl visit, but she decided to be placed with her sisters.

Milestone 47

About this time, a client of mine, who had become a friend, invited me to come and visit her in San Bernardino, CA. While visiting San Bernardino, I met her sister Peggy, who was the assistant director of Children's Village. She invited me to visit. Located in Beaumont, CA, It consisted of four double cottages, an administration building and a swimming pool. Each end of the cottages had four bedrooms and held 8-10 kids. The center of the cottages held showers bathrooms and a laundry room. The children, ages two to eighteen were all victims of abuse from LA County. Each one was sponsored by a movie star who kept track of the children, provided clothing, and gifts, etc. Peggy offered me a job as a counselor if I would move to San Bernardino.

By this time, I was becoming very unsettled by the type of creative finance we were involved in. Everyone was counting on the market changing so it would absorb the balloon payments we were sticking on the end of mortgages. I felt sure it was all going to tumble around our heels. Also my broker was crooked as a pretzel—there was something super slick about him and I wasn't too far off. He later became a used car salesman in Chico, CA. and sold me a string of cars that all broke down immediately after purchase. He finally went to prison for hiring someone to kill his second wife. She was a sweet lady who had five kids by her first husband.

His first wife was a really sweet lady and they had two kids together after I had quit the business. What a slime ball. To move to San Bernardino, I had to get rid of the house that I had bought. By this time KP and I had ripped out the horrible smelly carpets and refinished the floors. We had drained the swimming pool, thereby displacing the creature from the black lagoon, and filled it with clear sparkling water. We had trimmed the trees, including the loquat, apricot, and plum tree and manicured the yard. At the time, I had a number of clients, and in order to sell the house quickly, I used a technique I had learned in real estate school. I sold half of the house to a young couple who could not afford the entire price or the down payment, and the other half to an older couple who wanted an investment property.

The young couple paid half the house payment and half the rent. As a down payment, they rented a moving truck and moved me and KP to San Bernardino. My friend Patty had found us a place, so I moved right in and went to work at children's village the following week. I registered KP for high School and my friend Patty gave him a job as a busboy at the local country club. At Children's Village, later renamed, ChildHelp USA, we worked half a week. I went to work at noon on Sunday and got off at noon on Wednesday. My partner was a young 19 year-old guy from Beaumont. He was a nice kid, but not given to doing much work. The second half of the week was covered by a young woman (also from Beaumont) and a gay guy from LA who seemed pretty sure that he was practically perfect. She had a bad habit of giving the kids sugared cereal and candy treats on Sunday Morning.

By the time I got to work, they were bouncing off the walls as they were unused to that kind of diet. In my cottage, the first bedroom held three 10 and 11-year-old boys, the second held one two-year-old and two three-year-old boys. The third bedroom held a three-year-old girl and a 10-year-old girl. The fourth bedroom was empty. Cindy came shortly after I started working there. A social worker from LA brought her and sat her down on the counter where she sat, clutching her naked baby doll. He explained the child had been born in South Carolina and her parents had left her there when they had moved to California. They later had a baby boy and sent for her when she was two years old. The worker said that her parents had brought her to the welfare office, and said she was jealous, mean to the baby and unresponsive to them.

As he talked to the other counselors, I noticed that she was quietly whispering to her doll. Since it was lunch time, I asked her if she was hungry and she gave me a slight nod. I asked her if she would like a grilled cheese sandwich and milk and she gave me a slight smile. When she finished eating, I asked her if she would like to see her room and she took my hand and walked with me to her bedroom. It was a pretty room with pastel colors and a lot of stuffed animals sitting around. She looked so surprised; I don't know what she expected. I told her that the next day we would go out and buy her some clothes, since she came with nothing. I asked her if she would like to lie down for a while and she nodded, slipped her shoes off and laid down on the bed.

I covered her with a light blanket, kissed her on the forehead, and told her to call me if she needed me. As I walked out, I heard her whisper to her baby doll, "its ok baby, they haven't hit us yet."

Each counselor was specifically responsible for two kids. Tending to doctor's visits, school conferences and tending to any needed shopping. Since I was new, I was lucky enough to get Cindy and Joseph, the two-year-old boy. Cindy's movie star sponsors were Fred Mc Murray and June Haver. They were relatively new sponsors. They came out to meet Cindy and took her and me to lunch. They brought a carload of toys. June must have raided the local toy store for all the educational toys vetted for three-year-olds. Cindy was overwhelmed and spent most of her time snuggled in my lap. I adored Cindy and Joseph and would love to have adopted them. That, however, was against the policy of Children's Village. As counselors we needed to love them all.

My other brush with stardom came about when Children's Village held its annual guest party and chili cook off. Andy Granatelli's wife was the chili chef. Alana Ladd and Melissa Gilbert were there playing with the teenaged girls along with Rhonda Fleming-Mann and a dozen others—such nice caring people. The children were beside themselves with joy. The next event I was privileged to attend, along with KP, was the premier of the Burt Reynolds movie, "Paternity," at the Mann's Chinese theatre in Hollywood. Burt put his hands and boots in the concrete, June spotted KP and I and had Fred buy us popcorn and cokes. She introduced me to Rhonda Fleming, whom I had met at Children's Village, and it paid off big time.

Years later, Rhonda's son opened a theatre near Pittsburgh, CA where I had a foster home; I took my three older kids and went to the grand opening. Rhonda and her husband were there and she recognized me. She insisted on leading us around, filling our plates with goodies and gave me a glass of champagne. The kids got soda. She introduced me and the kids to her son and told him that the kids and I had free lifetime passes to his theatre. I worked at Children's Village for more than a year, and once again, got myself fired. A number of the children from the Village played Little League. One Saturday morning, I was transporting two of our boys and the older girl to the Little League field. Counselors from a nearby cottage asked me to take one of their boys too. Since my partner was late as usual, I had to take all eight of my kids plus the neighbor kid with me.

We watched the various games, had a snack, and generally enjoyed ourselves. When it was time to go, the boy from the other cottage was nowhere to be found. Thinking I had overlooked him in the crowd, I stayed for half an hour till the place was practically empty. Just then, a van from the Village pulled up beside me and they yelled, "We have him."

We immediately started back to the village. It was not my regular day to work. I had traded with someone because of Little League and so I was not aware of any appointments. The Little League field was in Cherry Valley and I had promised the children fresh cherries on the way home. When we arrived at the Village, I was met by a counselor who was angry because we were late. One of the three-year-old's mothers had come on a scheduled visit and had to wait half an hour for us.

On Monday, the director called me in and chastised me for being late. I explained that I felt I couldn't leave without the other boy, and he reminded me that I had stopped for the cherries, and therefore fired me.

Milestone 48

After signing up for unemployment, I decided to look for work in the area. I answered an ad for a group home in Rialto, the next town over. It turned out to be one of three group homes for dual diagnosed developmentally delayed people. The two houses in Rialto held either men or women. The third house, in Long Beach, was for children. After the interview with the director, they asked me if I would be willing to go to Long Beach. Since I felt that I would prefer being with children, I readily agreed. The shift was rather strange, requiring two days on, one day off, then three days on, two days off. The children were dual diagnosed, which means that in addition to having low mental function, they were diagnosed with varying degrees of a psychological condition, leaving them unbalanced. This meant they required constant highly attentive supervision. You never knew when one of them might misunderstand something and attack one of the children or a counselor. One little 12-year-old with beautiful blonde curls and the face of an angel, could explode like an atom bomb without warning.

I still carry scars from a couple of encounters with his fingernails. Yet, eventually, he became my very favorite and biggest success. There was also a 15-year-old autistic girl who was very sweet and lived in her own world populated with many imaginary friends and animals. There was a seven-year-old girl who had Cri du chat syndrome. This condition is recognized in infancy by the sounds the child makes that resembles the cry of a cat.

This angel had sharp features, slanted eyes and pointed ears. Her voice definitely sounded cat-like, though she spoke little. She was very sweet, never gave us a moment's trouble and we felt she was much smarter than she led us to believe. We had figured out that her parents had placed her with us because her father did not want her in the home. In retaliation she invariably pooped in her family's pool or living room when she went to visit. Nothing like that ever happened with us, though we took them swimming once a week.

I was assigned to CJ, the autistic boy, and worked with him, getting him to talk. He spoke American Sign Language rather fluently. However, he refused to make one sound. He loved to draw and often made very complicated structures. When we went to the park, he would not play with the others, but rather spent his time playing with a water fountain. One afternoon, we took them to the harbor to watch a sculling race. When we got home, CJ raced to his paper and pencil. He worked for about an hour and then brought me the paper. On one edge of the paper was a boat on water, on the other side was the water fountain. In between were a series of pipes, which I assumed, carried the water to the fountain.

CJ didn't realize that one couldn't drink ocean water and so he assumed that was what was coming from the water fountain. I showed it to a mechanic friend of mine and he was pretty sure it would have worked. CJ was an artistic and mechanical genius, trapped in an autistic body.

Milestone 49

I had developed the habit of calling my birth mother on Sundays. She lived with my aunt and was afflicted with emphysema. One Sunday, she couldn't come to the phone. When I asked why, my aunt, who was a devout Christian Scientist, hemmed and hawed and finally conceded that my mother was in the hospital. She told me that she would be home in a couple of days and that I should call back. I was not satisfied, and so I called the operator and got the number of the local hospital. I called the hospital and asked to speak to her. When she answered she sounded so weak.

She said she was so happy that I had called and that she had thought she would miss it. We chatted for a while and I told her that I loved her. Two days later, my aunt called me and told me she was gone. She told me that she had bought me a ticket on American Airlines and that my mother had left me a number of things and I should come to Oro Vista, Florida, where they lived. She said when I got there, we would collect the ashes and sprinkle them in the ocean, as Helen wanted.

From the very beginning it was one of the strangest experiences I'd ever had. It started on the plane when the stewardess asked me why I was going back east. I told her my mother had died and I was going back to be with my aunt, and help her deal with it. She smiled and said "that's nice, would you like a drink?"

She obviously hadn't paid attention. When my aunt picked me up, she explained that her son, Evan, my cousin, and his daughter Desirae had come for a long-planned vacation, and she didn't feel she could spoil it for them. So on the way home from the airport, we picked them up and went to Chuck E. Cheese's for dinner—I kid you not. The next day, we went to a Seminole village to watch them wrestle with alligators. The following day we went to Marine World to feed the dolphins and the day after we went to Silver Springs to ride boats. And so it went for the following days. I was there for two weeks in total.

At the end of the two weeks, since she had not received my mother's ashes, my aunt suggested that I go along home to California and that when she received them, she would sprinkle them herself at Daytona Beach as Helen had asked. She had helped me go through Helen's things. We shared her jewelry, she insisted I take a set of Noritake China, a dozen Hummel figurines, two government CDs and about $5000 cash. This was a fortune to me; I hadn't seen that much money in my life.

Milestone 50

When I returned to San Bernardino, I went back to work at the group home. CJ, the violent little autistic boy, jumped up the minute he saw me. He ran to me excitedly signing, "I love you," while making a sound in his throat like "uuuv ooo." He actually reached out, took hold of my arms and laid his cheek against my chest. I cried and so did he. It was as if he had cracked out of a shell. Gone was the angry boy. He looked at people, he interacted with the other kids and he tried to talk. He was so improved that when he went on a visit home, his parents decided to keep him.

With CJ gone, the house was not the same, and since I had enough money, I decided to make a change. I made arrangements to be a substitute in any of the three houses the doctor owned. I did it for a couple of months working mostly in the women's house and occasionally in the men's. I decided to make a change since they had dropped my wage from a decent level to minimum wage, since I was substituting. The other reason was that I was very frustrated by how the other counselors and housekeeping staff treated the clients. I knew I couldn't change human nature, and there is truth in the expression, power corrupts. My heart ached for how these helpless people were treated by some of the staff. I realized that the best thing I could do was get away.

Milestone 51

I decided to start my own foster home. Then I'd have no one to answer to and I would know how people were being treated. I was already licensed having worked in the group home and I thought it would be easy to get some clients. As it happened there were none available and so I signed up for the County foster home agency. Within a few days I was contacted regarding an emergency situation. Four kids, two brothers (12 and two years), and two other boys (10 and two years), had to be moved immediately – within the hour. A situation had occurred in their current foster home that required they be moved instantly.

They arrived within the hour, each clutching a pitiful bundle of clothes and looking shell shocked. The ten-year-old was quite slow and the two little ones were basically non-verbal. The twelve-year old, Ricky, was a most together young men. I later found out he had a reputation for being incorrigible and dangerous—I never saw it; it was baloney. Apparently when he was five years old, a teacher had insulted his mother and Ricky threw a chair at her (I know quite a few adults who might have responded in a like manner). As a result he'd been placed in a locked classroom for incorrigible kids ever since. When I went to enroll him for classes, I explained to them that he was perfectly fine. The superintendent argued with me at length, until he realized that Ricky was sitting quietly in the corner of the room during the entire session.

He called Ricky up, they had a conversation, and he assigned Ricky to a regular classroom. He proved his value a hundred times over to me. Once, I came outside to find him changing my tire. He hadn't even bothered to tell me, he just did it. His greatest triumph came when George (the 10-year-old) Ricky and I were shooting pool in the attached garage, the 2-year-olds had been tucked in bed for quite a while and were, we thought, sound asleep. Ricky had beaten me at 9-ball and so I had sent him inside to get us some sodas as a reward. He came flying out again, saying, "My god, Mom, you won't believe what my baby brother has done. I am afraid you will faint, Mom, I'm so glad it is you, my mother and that other lady would kill him."

I chuckled and said, "no killing in this house." I figured Ricky was over dramatizing some little thing—he wasn't. The two-year-olds (Robbie and Ryan) had managed to climb to the top of Ricky's dresser and get hold of a large new can of Cordovan Brown shoe polish. Using the polishing cloth and one of Ricky's socks, they had first polished each other head-to-toe and then the rest of the house from the level of the floor to about three feet up the walls.

The refrigerator, the dresser, the TV, the sofa, the bathtub and all the walls were smeared with Cordovan brown. George stared with his mouth hanging open, Ricky looked horrified, and the little ones looked proud of themselves. I didn't know whether to laugh or cry. Ricky said, don't worry mom, you take care of the babies, and I'll take care of the house, after scrubbing down the tub, so I could get close to it, I ran a bath and dunked my two little chocolate bars in the warm soapy water. I scrubbed and scrubbed, then drained and re-ran the bath and scrubbed again.

It was even inside their ears and between their toes!! By the time I had finished, they were exhausted (having missed their nap). So, I tucked them in and hoped that Robbie would be a house painter when he grew up, he was certainly thorough! By then Ricky had the house very much under control – almost three quarters done. In case you ever need to know, Kiwi shoe polish comes off easily with hot soapy water. Just another day in a mother's life. Shortly after that, circumstances sent the kids back to their mothers and I moved on.

Milestone 52

Since the act of substituting had pleased me, I decided to become a substitute teacher in the school district. Even in those days, the pay was $80 per day. All one had to do was pass the CBEST test and sign up at the local school headquarters. The nice thing about it was that you could pick your days, call in and pick your class. I still bowled on Wednesdays. Take my advice, never sign up for a Junior High school class. The rowdy little demons will eat you alive. High schoolers will ignore you; those classes are a good place to catch up on your reading. The little kids are great fun, but my favorites were the disabled kids. One room held four kids in comas. All one did there was change the music and keep the lights and pictures flashing and watch for signs of consciousness. The room I worked most had 3 eight year-old boys and one girl.

One boy was quadriplegic, one had cerebral palsy and one was deaf mute. When they came in the morning, the driver of the bus would lay the quadriplegic boy on his tummy just outside the door to the classroom. The two other boys would lay down beside him with their arms at their side, the quadriplegic boy would start jerking his head in such a way that he would move forward a few inches, the other boys would do the same thing, and they would all squirm into the classroom.

We lifted little Joey into a wheel chair that he could move by blowing into a tube and the other two boys sat in their seats. The little girl watched them, giggling, she didn't seem to have a disability and I didn't want to ask. Since most substitute teachers would not go there, I spent many of my days with these kids. One day, after a couple of months, the little girl jerked, fell from her seat and went into a violent seizure. I was told that she had an inoperable brain tumor and would not be with us much longer.

Milestone 53

When summer came, there were no jobs for substitutes. Perusing the paper, I came across an ad in the paper for a position as a counselor for visiting Japanese students. I was invited to a meeting in Rialto, and discovered that over 200 students would be spending the summer in the area. As counselors, we were supposed to find the students places to live in private homes. We were supposed to teach classes four mornings a week with a couple of excursions and save our Wednesdays for one big trip.

Wednesdays were to include a trip to Disneyland, all day at Perris Lake, a Baseball game, and the La Brea Tar Pits and China Town. The company paid for all excursions, plus provided a budget to spend any way we wanted on the kids. Since I belonged to the Science of Mind church, I convinced members of the congregation to take in my 30 students. I hired my best friend Mike as my assistant. It was great fun. One afternoon, I took them to Lake Arrowhead Hilton Hotel restaurant. I introduced them to my son KP who was working as a breakfast chef, They all fell in love with his 6"4", frame, dimples and the cleft in his chin. They thought his green eyes were amazing.

All except Chenaboo , the only boy, who was checking out the waitresses. We went on the boat ride around the lake and then went ice-skating. I told them that quite a few Olympic stars practice at that rink and they were very impressed. Another afternoon, we were swimming at Perris Lake and I ordered two 6' long sandwiches from Subway. The kids loved it. These kids all went to a Buddhist school on Hamamatsu on the southern end of Japan. They told me that the climate was similar to San Bernardino, that they raise oranges there and that they have their own theme park on the lake. They were a great bunch of kids, I liked them all and I had a really nice time.

Milestone 54

The following school year was going well until I got a phone call from my mother. She said that my father was blind and on a walker, and that she was half blind and hardly able to get around. She said that she had fallen, torn all the cartilage loose in her sternum, and moving was terribly painful. She asked me to please come home and help her deal with Dad. I called KP and we were on a plane by 2 o' clock that afternoon. I never went back to live in San Bernardino.

As it happened it took until the middle of January before I could leave my folks. My father was extremely resistant about going to a convalescent home. KP and I went to all of them in the area and found a lovely place that had just built on a new wing. We discussed, described, begged and pleaded, but it wasn't until after Christmas that we finally came to an understanding. KP had returned to San Bernardino right after Christmas. I asked my father "Do you want me to move here? I'll send for my dogs and my things?"

He said, "No! I want to stay here as long as we can!"

I said, "Dad, you have, and you are killing this woman" (indicating my mother). The next morning, with Dad in an ambulance and mom in my car, we went off to Janie's Nursing home. My folks had a beautiful room together with a window onto a quiet shady street. They were ten feet from the dining room door and about 15 feet from the front desk and the door to outside.

Because they were both mentally competent they had the option of calling a cab and going downtown. Mom loved Dairy Queen and in the summer, a couple of times a week, she would call a cab and go to Dairy Queen to get a blizzard. My father had worn only pajamas for years, but they said that he must dress. So I bought him 3 sweat suits and some crazy tee-shirts. He loved them. The man across the hall had been an usher at their wedding. They knew many of the staff who treated them like royalty. My Dad admitted that he wished he had come there years before.

I had gone to visit them both in the summer, but had to return in October when my father passed away. My father passed only a week after my parent's 62nd wedding anniversary. As it happened, mother and father were very well known in our small town. So, the various organizations: Kiwanis, Lions Club and American Legion, wanted to do something to honor them. In recognition of my parent's contribution to the community, these groups combined resources and put a flagpole and a plaque in front of the convalescent home where they resided.

American Legion established a scholarship in my father's name for young people attending Girl or Boys State. They had a huge open house with champagne and cocktails. However by this time, my father was too ill to get out of bed. In less than a week, he was dead. At Thanksgiving, my cousin Denney had a big party and included my mother in the festivities. She passed away two weeks later. They are the only two people I know who both had going away parties. I hope I am as lucky.

Milestone 55

Since I inherited everything there was, and having not returned to San Bernardino, I bought a house in Pittsburg, CA. A friend of mine, with KP, collected all my things and moved everything up north for me. I looked up an old friend of mine who happened to be the number two person in social services in San Francisco. She talked me into opening a foster home and facilitated the quick procurement of my license. Since I had cleaned out my parents' home and had loaded all I could use into a moving van, I was open and running within three weeks. My first foster kids were two Native American kids, a four- year-old boy and his two-year old sister. The things these two beautiful children had been subjected to would break your heart.

Despite all that, they were sweet and loving kids who loved to laugh, sing and dance. The boy in particular, had an absolutely exquisite voice. Years later when they came by to visit, he told me he was a member of the San Francisco Boys Chorus. As a teen he was adopted by a family in Utah. I wonder if he became part of the Mormon Tabernacle Choir. As there was not as big a need in Contra Costa County as there was in San Francisco, my San Francisco friend sent me some of their children. One evening I took one of the kids to the shelter home building in San Francisco for a visit.

Milestone 56

As I walked around the corner to get a cup of tea I ran into the cutest little kid. He was a tiny little Latino boy with creamy tanned skin, long curly brown hair and a grin as wide as the Mississippi River. Wearing a torn tank top, he had dirt smudges on his face and burns and scabs on his body. I later counted 35 old and new cigarette burns on him. It turned out that his mother, often high on drugs or alcohol, would burn him accidentally when she gestured with a cigarette in her hand. Then, he looked to be about 18 months old, and he walked towards me with his hands lifted, asking thereby to be picked up. When I picked him up, He threw his arms around me and snuggled his head into my shoulder. I was immediately in love. I said, "I am not sure, but I think I just picked up an elf, and I want it."

One worker said, "Oh he is already scheduled for Millbrae," (a nearby town).

At the same time, the directors voice came floating out of her office, and she said, "if that is Sue Handley, give her anybody she wants."

This was November and it was cold in San Francisco and my little buddy felt cold. I knew they had a closet there filled with children's clothes for such emergencies and so I found pants, a shirt, and a jacket for him. It was then I learned he had a 3 year old brother. I was only licensed for five and even though I had a sixth bed, they wouldn't let me take his brother at the same time.

They said that he would have to go to Millbrae for that week, but since I had an opening on Wednesday, they would bring his brother over then. The older boy Joey cried and begged me not to take little John. It broke my heart. I explained that he would be reunited with his brother in just a few days and they would live together with me, but a three-year-old really doesn't understand such things.

Over the years, I had managed to collect four dogs—two little cockapoos, one half coyote/half cocker spaniel, and one half Great Dane and half German Shepard. The next week, when the doorbell rang, the German Shepard came with me to open the door. There stood Joey and the social worker, Francie. The Great Dane mix was face to face with Joey. She gave him a lick and he jumped and started screaming, absolutely terrified. I knew I had to do something fast, and so I scooped him up to the back porch where the other kids were.

We had three bouncy houses and an old sofa on the porch (which the kids were allowed to jump on) and there was little Johnny, joyously using it as a trampoline. Joey's eyes got as big as dollars. He said, "Jumping on the furniture, are you going to hit him?"

I said, "We don't hit here. He's having fun, its ok." I set him on his feet and within 10 minutes he was jumping away with his brother John. It turned out later that Joey had been trained as a thief. Once we stopped at a convenience store so I could get some diapers.

Joey said, incredulously, "Did you pay for those, Mom?" Then he told me that he should have knocked down a big pile of cans that were pyramid style. Then he suggested that while he and the shop keeper were picking up the cans, I could have grabbed the diapers and run out of the store. Later, when we were giving another boy a ride home from visitations, he proudly explained to him, "we did not steal or hit in this family."

At the time, I had a beautiful five-year old African American girl, and a mixed race four-year-old boy staying with me in addition to Joey and John. Along about February, that boy was adopted out and I received a seven-month-old African American baby girl, Jeanna. Other kids came and went, but Joey, John, and Jeanna seemed to be with me permanently. Sure enough, two years later, the boys' social worker asked if I would like to adopt them. He said that there was no way for them to return to their biological parents and that there was no adoption demand for Hispanic boys. I said that I would like to, but that I didn't know how I would be able to support them. He explained that Nancy Reagan had set up a fund for exactly that purpose. He said that it would be a check, just like fostering and I wouldn't have to worry about anything.

Since I already adored the boys, I said, "yes, of course." The following week, Jeanna's social worker said, "I hear you are adopting Joe and John, do you want to adopt Jeanna too?"

I said, I thought that cross-racial adoption wasn't allowed. She responded, Oh, yes, Nancy Reagan wants you to, she thinks it will help end prejudice."

Of course, I was crazy about Jeanna, and said, "Anything for Nancy Reagan. Even if I am Democrat."

She said, "Great. There are 72 African American kids awaiting adoption, and only three families have expressed interest." At that time, something changed in my attitude, I am sure that the children saw nothing different, but I felt that no longer did I have to fear that the kids I loved so much would be taken away without warning. I had left Cindy and Joey at children's village and other children I loved had come and gone. Each time a child leaves, they take a piece of your heart with them. I was elated not to have to face that again until the bombshell hit.

They sent me a letter saying I could not adopt Jeanna because it was against San Francisco's policy. It turned out her worker was totally Looney Tunes and had been taken out of the office on a gurney. By this time however, they were my kids and I decided to fight. We were arguing with the office when my friend who had facilitated my license phoned me. She gave me the name of an attorney who had once worked for social services, she said that he "knew where the bodies were buried," and that though he would charge me, he would zero the bill out and call it uncollectable.

I went to see him, and he asked "so you want to adopt three drug babies?" I don't know if you are crazy or a glutton for punishment." He said, "It's time San Francisco's social services joined the 21st century, so let's do it!" It was not long after that that I was informed that Jeanna had a little brother, Joshua, and did I want him? It required moving one little two-year-old foster boy that I had, but I said, Yes, lets do it. So now I had four kids that I was fighting to adopt, Joe, John, Jeanna, and Joshua.

Milestone 57

At this time, there was a TV show in San Francisco called "People Are Talking." Because of my fight to adopt my kids, I was invited to be on the show. For the show, they assembled a panel that consisted of myself, two other white women from Contra Costa County who wanted to adopt black children, a white woman with a black teenaged adopted daughter who loved her family situation, a white woman with an older Alaskan native American adopted daughter, who while she loved her adoptive mother wanted to return to Alaska and her tribe, and Ann Davis, director of San Francisco social services. Sitting in the front row, directly in front of me was a black social worker who insisted that white people couldn't understand the black experience. Being frustrated with her heckling, I responded to something the woman said, "In foster parent orientation, we are told that we must be "colorblind." I am colorblind, and now they are telling me that I am the wrong color."

We went to commercial and Russ McEwen leaned over and said, "I wish you'd speak your mind Sue, stop being such a wilting violet." Everyone laughed. Shortly after we resumed, a call came in from Hunters Point, a largely African American area of greater San Francisco. Referring to an earlier comment, the caller said, "If she can't do their hair, I'll do it for her. It is obvious that she loves those kids and they couldn't have a better home."

Within two weeks after the program aired, I dreamed that Jeanna had another baby brother. When the call came the next day from a social worker friend of mine, I was not surprised. She said, guess who has a new brother?" and I said, "Jeanna and Joshua."

When I told her I had dreamed it she told me I was weird and asked if I wanted him. I said, "Of course." She said, not so fast, they think he is profoundly retarded and may never be able to walk or talk and he may have cerebral palsy. I said, "so what, he is their brother, bring him over!"

And with that James was added to our family. I remember that they had told me that Jeanna was retarded and it turned out that she was deaf. One look at her bright eyes and sweet smile told me that she was not slow. Since I had worked with deaf kids, I recognized the situation and fortunately knew sign language. She had easily learned basic sign and by the time she was two, communicated easily and constantly with me and the boys. As it turned out James was certainly not retarded and there was no sign of cerebral palsy. Basically, he did not relate to strangers and rarely bothered to communicate. I had a young teenaged helper who spent much of her time with James.

Once when he was about two years old, she was holding him, she asked if I was going to take J-I-M with me, he smiled and said "J-I-M, that's me."

About that time social services decided to torpedo me once and for all. They sent a black sociologist over to do a bonding study, thinking I would fail. This sociologist was known to be quite opposed to cross-racial adoption. He came three times and talked to the kids and me on various topics.

The final time he came, my four oldest kids were in school, or Headstart. It was near lunchtime and I had just put James in the highchair with his food. The doctor and I chatted while James ate. When he was finished, I washed his hands and face and he got down from the chair and crawled up on my lap. He was fussing a bit and squirming around and I observed "It's this guy's naptime, if you'll excuse us. James, tell the man bye-bye."

James waved bye-bye and I carried him to his bed tucked him in with his favorite blanket, and turned the music box on. When I came back and sat down, the doctor was staring into space, and listening hard for something. He said, "did you give him a bottle?"

I said, "No. I wean kids at 15 months. I started it with my 20 year old son (KP), and it works just fine."

He said, "but he's not crying."

I asked, "Why should he cry? He's tired and wants a nap." He seemed totally amazed and soon left. We had one more occasion when I threw a party for all my friends of various backgrounds and invited the doctor. There were black, white, Hispanic, and mixed kids, and their parents from my original day nursery. One black man, a deacon of the Science of Mind church we belonged to, said to the doctor, "If she doesn't adopt these kids, they will end up being shuttled from foster home to foster home until they end up in Folsom Prison." The rest of them got on the band wagon and the poor doctor was besieged. He finally said, "Whoa, wait, I am totally on her side. I've seen enough, these kids are definitely her children. To remove them now would be psychologically very damaging to them."

A week later, a letter came from social services. Obviously, they did not want to lose face. The letter read, "It is San Francisco's policy not to allow cross-racial adoption. However, since your home consists of 2 Hispanics, 3 African Americans and 1 white it is a 'house of color.' The adoption may be finalized. Please present yourself to the court house in Contra Costa County on October 19, 1990 at 9 am. The judge will finalize the adoption and present you with five birth certificates listing you as mother."

I cried, my helper cried, soon the kids cried and then we were all crying and laughing. I kept telling the kids, "You're mine, all mine." They didn't understand because as long as they could remember, they had always been mine.

Milestone 58

During that time, because I received funding from the Aid to Adoptive Parents Grant, I got to be a stay- at-home parent. As a youngster, I had always loved the book, "The Five Little Peppers and How They Grew" by Margaret Sidney, which depicts the busy life of a household with five children. My life was similarly busy. I had very little time for myself. My teenage helper's mother Barbara (who was also a lesbian) had showed interest in me, but I just didn't have time. My friend Marty Coe who everything started from, had by this time moved to Willows, CA.

She came down every month or so and spent a weekend with me, and that was the extent of my social life. Three kids in diapers, a hyperactive three-year-old, and a busy four-year-old will do that to you. The one escape I had was with Cindy Steen and her lover, Carolyn. After reading for Jack a number of times and even on a trip to Indiana, reading for Cindy again, Cindy and Carolyn decided to move to California. Cindy had brought her teenage daughter along and Carolyn had brought her 4-year-old son, Scott.

We spent a lot of time together at each other's homes, playing cards, etc. When he was about seven years old, we attended Scotty's soccer game, Joe was so excited about the game that I signed him up the next year, along with his brother John. Joe was a natural athlete and played all the way through high school. Joe's first love was actually baseball and he also played every all-star game they had for kids and beyond. John, unfortunately, had binocular vision. This means that he only looked out of one eye at a time. His depth perception was askew and that meant that he was not good at team sports. However, he excelled at gymnastics and diving.

Milestone 59

In 1991, when Joe was eight and John, seven and Jeanna, Josh and Jimmy, six, five, and four, Marty Coe offered to rent us her parents' home in Willows; her folks had just gone into a convalescent home. We moved just at the beginning of Little League season, and Joe and John loved it. In the fall I saw a sign on TV for soccer signups in Chico and since there was no soccer in Willows, I took the kids over to sign them up.

Driving all five kids to various practices during the week and games on Saturday nearly bled me dry financially. Unfortunately there was no place in Willows where John could be trained in gymnastics and swimming and I could not afford more trips back and forth to Chico where the closest training was. The years passed quickly. Much time was spent camping, I was a member of Thousand Trails, we made yearly trips to Disneyland and the kids played all kinds of sports. We loved Willows and the kids made lots of friends. Before I knew it Joe and John were in High School and Jeanna was getting ready to start freshman year.

Jeanna's debut in sports was definitely an experience. At her level teams were a mix of boys and girls. There was only one other girl on the soccer team who apparently fell in love with my (then) 4-year-old Jeanna. The team was known as the "Headbangers" although they were not allowed to use headers at this level. The coaches apparently were unaware of this. The coaches, a couple of 30-ish men, were only interested in their sons and the boys on the team. They totally ignored the girls. Jeanna's little friend spent all of her time hanging on Jeanna and wanting to play ring-around-the-rosy. After two games of watching the girls dancing together at one end of the field and the boys scoring at the other, I decided to take a hand.

At the end of each game, a parent brought a treat for the team. At this particular game, they were beautiful decorated cupcakes. When Jeanna went to get one, I stopped her and told her that she was not allowed to have one. She looked horrified and asked why. I explained that the treats were for the players only. I said, "you girls didn't play soccer, you may have some milk and crackers at home."

My daughter whimpered all the way home, nearly breaking my heart. The next game, she shook the girl off and spent most of her time in the middle of the pack and even scored twice. From that time on Jeanna was a super athlete, even taking the role of sweeper in most soccer games. She was also outstanding in Little League and became a super softball player. I have no doubt that Jeanna would have become a scholarship baby given half a chance.

Milestone 60

Her potential career was tragically cut off on November 25, 2001. It was dusk and she had decided to run over to a girlfriend's house only a few blocks away. It was growing quite dark and even though she had glowing stripes down her pant legs and jacket sleeves, a truck came around a corner and struck her. Jeanna was knocked 25 ft. down the road, was scraped bruised and unconscious. The young man driving had just picked up one of Joshua's friends to babysit for him. She called me immediately and I rushed over. The EMTs told me that they would be taking Jeanna by helicopter to Enloe Hospital in Chico. The young woman later told me that the young man and she had been looking at each other and laughing about something, they didn't see Jeanna until they hit her. That was the end of Jeanna's blazing speed and she never made it back to high school.

We did home school after that. She spent a week in the Hospital and had only been home a week when we went to the mall to do Christmas shopping. Joshua pushed her all over the place in a wheel chair, and I told them to pick their favorite Christmas gift and get it. I don't remember what Jeanna got, but Joshua wanted a Playstation from the pawn shop. We went to the food court for lunch to decide exactly what we were going to do next. Joe and John had chosen video games, James wanted shoes, but they were twice the amount I had budgeted for them.

We decided that Jeanna, Joshua and I would go to the pawn shop to get Joshua's Playstation, while Joe and John stayed in the arcade and Jimmy looked for shoes within his budget. Joshua kept complaining of being thirsty, so we grabbed some bottled water and headed to the pawn shop. Once there, he found exactly what he wanted and even had enough for some games to go with it. Before the sale was complete he changed his mind and said, "Never mind Mom, lets go back to the mall." When I asked him why, He said, "I am grown up. Jimmy is just a kid," (though there was only 14 months difference in their age) "lets give him my money so he can get his shoes, I can wait."

I asked him if he was really sure and he insisted that was exactly what he wanted to do. I was so proud of him. When we got back he found his little brother and off they went to the shoe store. The shoes were bright blue, and I thought, a bit funny looking, but Jimmy was delighted and so was Joshua. This was not the only time that Joshua stepped forward to be the family hero. He was a very large boy. He stood a head taller than me and was quite heavy. He was a super soccer goalie and his baseball team called him "old homerun."

His strength was never so obvious or important when one evening in July I had a fainting spell. I had had these strange little fainting spells frequently, just as I was about to lie down at night. They had been variously diagnosed as sinus infection, epilepsy or anxiety. One doctor in the Willows emergency told me it was "the vapors," and all in my head, and I should never come back and bother them. On this particular occasion, it was the worst that I had ever had.

As usual, when I started to faint, I yelled for the boys, three or four minutes later when I came to, Joe and Joshua were standing over me. While unconscious, I had messed myself, so I immediately headed for the shower. Joshua informed me that they were taking me to the ER, whether I wanted to go or not.

As I got out of the shower, he covered his eye with one hand and handed me clean shorts with the other, and then he backed out, and using the same process, handed me a clean shirt. He then, put his arm around me, and half-carried me to the car. A different doctor was on duty at the hospital, and after a few minutes of trying to explain what was going on, they rushed me into one of the exam rooms. I was immediately surrounded by people, someone putting in an IV, another taking my blood pressure while others made observations about my situation. At one time, I lost consciousness and when I came to, the doctor was standing there with paddles in his hands. "I was out" I said.

"We noticed" he responded, then laughed. They put a strange contraption on my chest that was thumping like a heartbeat. I later found out that the contraption was called an external pacemaker. Suddenly, they were taking everything off me and new people in green were putting new ones on.

"We are sending you to Enloe Hospital in a helicopter," the doctor told me.

"Can't" my son just drive me? Please?" I begged. "I don't want to go in a helicopter."

Joe said, "Suck it up Marine, that's the way you are going." The helicopter makes it from Willows to Chico in the time it takes to say the 23rd Psalm, two-and-a-half times.

In Chico, they gave me a pacemaker and sent me home in great shape, no more fainting spells. That was 17 years ago, and I've been fine since, but if Joshua had not pushed me to go to the hospital that day, I would not be here today. I later found out Joshua stopped a fight in his school between a big girl and a sweet racially mixed little Philippino girl. The big girl had a vicious reputation. Joshua told her, "to leave the kid alone or she would answer to him," and she backed down. He then walked the girl home; just to be sure the girl would be okay.

When he got there, her mother was mowing the front yard, He told her, "you take care of your daughter, and I will mow the lawn." Her mother told me about it much later. That and many similar stories emerged about Joshua in the coming months. The Saturday after the mall trip to pick out Christmas presents, Joshua asked if he could skip his chores, saying that he didn't feel well and promising to make up for it later.

I said, "of course," because he had always been my primary helper. He'd help put groceries away, help me cook, and made me tea without being asked. And during most of all that, he would be singing. He had a sweet, pure tenor voice that made Michael Jackson sound like a crow. On Sunday, Joshua still felt bad. I offered to take him to the emergency room with me as I had a cramp in my neck that I wanted to get a shot for.

He refused to go, saying that he just wanted to rest. When I came home, I asked him how he was, and he said that he was okay. I told him that I loved him and he said, "I love you too, Mom."

Milestone 61

I went to bed. The next morning, Josh wouldn't wake up. We called 911. When they arrived, the EMTs said his blood sugar was off the scale. They flew him to Chico in the helicopter and Jeanna and I followed as fast as we could in the car. The doctor at Enloe told me not to worry. "People did not die from high blood sugar." He said he was coming in and out of consciousness, and that they were going to do one more test to make sure that nothing else was going on, so I should relax. I went to get a shot in my back, since the muscle had cramped up again, when I heard them calling code blue.

It meant nothing to me until a nurse came to me and said to come with her, that Joshua had crashed. They made me wait in a waiting room down the hall and wouldn't let me and Jeanna near him. They said they were testing his blood gasses and the next thing I knew; they were telling me he was gone. A couple of months before, he and his friend, Cheeto, had bleached their hair. The nurse offered to cut me a lock of his hair to have, but I said no, he didn't like his hair disturbed in anyway and liked it the way it was. Jeanna and I kissed him and walked out. I was speechless and devastated.

As we got to the elevator, the door opened and John Duncan and his son Morgan stepped out. The Duncan's were a Willows family with five children, the same ages as mine. The Duncan kids were mixed race and were very close to my kids. It turned out that John(Handley), being at the Duncan house, had called the hospital to see how Joshua was. The woman at the desk, asked if he was a relative, and when John said yes, she told him, "oh, he died."

John, only 15 at the time, nearly fainted and so Karen Duncan (John Duncan's wife) took over the phone. When she discovered what happed, she called her husband, who happened to be in Chico and told him to go to the hospital and meet us. That is why John stepped out of the elevator. He took us in hand and insisted on driving us home in my car. When we got home, she had James and John calmed down and had fixed dinner for all of us.

The following year was an absolute haze. I was in such pain, I wanted to die too, but knew I couldn't because I had the other kids. I still miss him every day and each morning think, "Oh god, another day without Joshua." Enough time has passed, and I've heard enough of those stories that I've realized that Joshua was an angel and had accomplished what he was sent here to do. Jeanna and James insisted on homeschooling from then on and were very reclusive, especially for the first year.

Over the next four years, Jeanna was in and out of one scrape or another, but she finally settled. James met a young woman over the internet and became involved, the result was a beautiful son named Stephon. That relationship was doomed from the start because James was so reclusive that he never wanted to go out and do anything.

Finally, Stephon's mother took him to Fairfield to be near the rest of the family and we never get to see him as none of us drive. In the meantime, John got involved with an absolutely gorgeous Native American girl named Romelia. Together, they produced Jordan, the brightest, most handsome, and talented grandchild, two years older than Stephon. John, although trained as a barber, became a well-known tattoo artist in Chico and Willows. He and Romelia produced Julian, a darling little spitfire, who is currently five. Jeanna got married, and she and her husband fell in love with Stephon and within a year, had a baby boy named Alexander.

About three years later they presented me with my first granddaughter, Jasmine. Joe, the oldest, had gone in the Navy at 19. When he completed his tour of duty, he got involved with sheet metal work in San Francisco and rarely saw us. In January 2018, Joe and his girlfriend Tanya produced Maylena, one of the most beautiful baby girls. Isn't it interesting that all of my grandchildren turned out to be the cutest and smartest children in the world. What are the odds??

Book 4

Relentlessly Gay

I had gone through a number of frustrating situations with my parents and my cousin Joanne. When, for one reason or another, I refused to do something that would have been very good for them. After these occasions, I swore that I would never refuse to do what a number of well-meaning people encouraged me to do. As a result, much to my disgust, I felt I had to see a counselor after I lost my Josh. I knew in my heart that I wouldn't like it and that it wouldn't help, but I had promised. I was doubly annoyed when the local mental health office assigned me to a male counselor. I gritted my teeth and walked into his office with a chip the size of the Empire State building on my shoulder.

Milestone 62

My counselor, Dale, was a good-looking soft-spoken man around 40. I don't remember what he said to me, but my first words were (angrily) "I'm a lesbian." I waited for his reaction—there was none. He quietly asked, "Is that a problem for you?"

I responded, "No! of course not."

He said, "Good, my girlfriend is a lesbian, except when she is with me. You'd like her." Then he asked me about Joshua. I explained that my heart was broken, and that I would never be able to get over his loss, no matter what. He said gently, "Of course not, no one ever does. All I can do is give you some strategies to help you cope."

I confess, by this time, he had begun to win me over.

Medical allows eight weeks per person of that sort of counseling. We started with Jeanna, who came maybe three times out of the eight. Next, Joe came and stayed once and the other remaining kids stayed a few times each. Off and on between sessions, he would bring me back for another eight weeks. Before I knew it, a year had gone by. I looked forward to my weekly meetings with my counselor. We laughed, cried and shared all kinds of stories. As promised he even sent his girlfriend to visit me in the hospital and as he predicted, I really liked her. We even met a couple of times in Chico at The Upper Crust, by "accident."

Milestone 63

I said one day, I felt compelled to say "I hate to say this, but as much as I like seeing you and enjoy spending time with you, I really don't need you anymore." He said, "that is true, but now, I need you and I have one more role to complete. That is to reunite you with your people. For the last 15 years you have given 100 percent of your life to your children. Joe is in the Navy, John is in Barber College, Jeanna is off with her boyfriend, and James really doesn't need you anymore, It is time you went back to your people."

"Easier said than done I stammered, there's not much of a gay community in Willows."

He said, "that is true but Chico has a Stonewall Alliance. The women's gay chorus, the women's monthly potluck and a gay bar. You need to get involved." I was amazed. I didn't quite know which way to turn. He said, "my girl Kay sometimes goes to the women's potluck, I will get you the details." It turned out that the potlucks were the first Saturday of the month at various women's homes. He made me promise that I'd go. When I did, I must admit that walking into that house alone, knowing no one, was one of the scariest things I have ever done. Once inside, I was welcomed by a lovely older lady who started introducing me around. There were around 30 or 40 women of all walks, from the very stylish made up feminine types to the stomping "diesel" dyke in boots and tie.

Everyone was talking, laughing and joking and having a good time. I wandered around a bit and finally was invited to join a table of five other women in the back yard. They turned out to be academic types, three instructors from local colleges and one high school teacher. It didn't take long before we were all friends. The potlucks quickly became an integral part of my life. As my social life got better, my physical health was getting worse. I was diagnosed with COPD – I'd been a heavy smoker until 1972 when KP asked me to stop. Before long the trips to Enloe hospital came too frequently. Since all the kids were out of school James and I decided to move to Chico.

Milestone 64

With the success of the potlucks in mind, I decided to visit the Stonewall alliance office. I found they were looking for volunteers to "man" the office in the afternoons and so I volunteered for Tuesdays and Thursdays. My partner was a man close to my age with some physical limitations. He wanted to retire, but we had been just been given a grant of 2000 books on gay subjects, between the two of us, we separated the books into subjects and then alphabetized them by author. I then went through the women's novels and divided them by genre. I decided I wanted to read my way through them. I started with the Sci-Fi and went on to the mysteries. I was almost through when this straight woman that served on the board came in one afternoon and told me that I was fired.

She said, "You are going blind, we can't use you anymore."

I was very upset, took my things and walked out. It didn't take me long to discover that I was not the first to be treated in such a shabby manner. Now almost eight years later, I understand via the grape vine that Stonewall is in turmoil again. Oh well, despite the pain, two really good things came out of my work at Stonewall. One afternoon, a young woman sporting a Mohawk and several decorative bits of metal in her face showed up. She said she was a Vista volunteer from Minnesota, stationed in Chico. She was a cute little 20-year- old, full of energy and fun, and her name was Cassie. She wanted to know all about the gay community in Chico.

Milestone 65

On a related tangent, the second blessing that I learned of through my volunteer work at Stonewall was the Imperial Sovereign Court of the Czaristic Dynasty. It's a group of (mostly) drag queens who belong to related drag performance chapters all over the country. It was started by a drag queen from San Francisco called Mother Jose' Sierra. A few years ago she was called to the great "gay bar in Valhalla" but the shows go on and her legacy remains. The shows are put on once a month to raise money for charity and to illustrate the valuable contributions that the GLBTQA+ community can make to society. As it happened there was a show scheduled for the following Saturday and I invited my new friend Cassie to go with me.

I had discovered that if you volunteered to set up and clean up, you did not need to pay the $10 donation to enter—an important consideration since my only income was social security and not a whole lot at that. One of my partners at Stonewall, a young man named Shen, agreed to go with me also and help set up. Cassie was a volunteer bartender while Shen and I set up tables and chairs and helped with the decorating. This worked well through the reigns of two Empresses. The first empress was Desirae.

Milestone 66

Claudette De Versace, the original founder and empress was elected for a second reign, the second year that I attended. Shen and Cassie had become like adopted kids and Claudette like a big sister. During the first reign, we talked Shen into trying drag. He was very awkward at first, breaking a heel the night of his first performance. By our second year, with his mother sewing his clothes and Claudette teaching him makeup, he had become extremely proficient. When crowned, Claudette De Versace named Shen princess and me royal Duchess. Shen performed in every show and got better and better. We knew one day he would be Empress in his own right, which happened a few years later. I sometimes read Tarot cards at the back of the room , but didn't perform (as 'Suzette La Dyke') until many years later. My friend Starla (aka 'Bela La Ball) and I performed a rendition of "That Old Black Magic."

That performance took place at a Cinco de Mayo party thrown by my friend, Bob, a former Emperor from Stockton who was famous in the drag community for his parties. When there was a call for help for his parties I volunteered. We hit it off perfectly, and over the years his best buddy David and I became known as "the gay musketeers." We attended all court functions, hit the casinos and generally hung out together. David stood up with Bob when he married his husband Nathan and I performed the hand fasting portion of the ceremony.

Bob's "kids" (dogs Toto and Cha-cha) were the ring bearers and were led down the aisle at the right moment. Bob's husband, Nathan, joined us in our escapades whenever he could and together we had a wonderful time. When we lost David a few years ago, it broke our hearts. It's never been quite the same since. As it happened, without Bob, I too would have passed and he saved my life a few years later.

Milestone 67

After that time, Cassie became my sidekick. My vision was deteriorating and I began to let her do all the driving. At this particular time, James had met a young woman online and they became involved. The result was my grandson Stephon. Cassie, who was really great with kids, often took him along with us when we went out. Marty Coe had passed away from lung cancer shortly before we left Willows. Cassie seemed to step in and take her place.

Cassie went to work for an organization called Passages, first as a volunteer and then as a regular employee when her time with Vista was up. Passages has a mission of helping older adults in many capacities. They advise seniors concerning Medicare, housing, food, etc. They also arrange for rides and provide visiting companions who visit seniors weekly. Cassandra insisted on setting me up with a psychologist, even though I told her it was not necessary. She explained that she needed the numbers to meet her quotas at work and so I agreed.

Milestone 68

When Laura, the director, and a psychologist named "Bink" came over they decided after an hour that I truly did not need one. Then Laura said that since this was Bink's first time working with seniors, would I mind letting her come over, just to get the feeling for it? They said that since I was a pagan lesbian and totally unorthodox it would be an interesting experience for Bink. I had liked the small woman immediately, and so I agreed.

She was kind, sweet, curious, and quite understanding, with a wonderful sense of humor. The goal was to match me with a senior companion, which turned out to not be as easy as it sounds. They finally sent one woman over who spent one visit with me. She later said that she could deal with the lesbian, but not the pagan who has an altar to Yemanja in her living room.

Some time passed before they found someone else, a woman named CJ, who said that she didn't think she could deal with it, but she'd give it a shot. As it happened, she was a perfect fit; in no time at all I loved her like a sister. She claimed to be a good Baptist, but believed god was a spaceman (with which I agree). She was at that time, carrying on online with someone who claimed to be an Englishman who was madly in love with her.

We laughed about it and wondered how long it would take before he asked her for money. It took less time than we thought. Somehow the poor fellow, got left in Hong Kong when his boat sailed without him. His money was tied up in England and he only needed a few thousand to be able to come here and be with her. Ha-ha. CJ and I continued to see each other weekly for years and our friendship is still rock-solid.

Milestone 69

During the time in which I was reading my way through the Stonewall library, I came across a book called "Blue: A novel" by Abigail Padgett. In it, the author mentions that the labrys, was once the symbol of the women's liberation movement. The labrys – a double headed axe, was said to be the ceremonial tool of the goddess. It was worn by supporters of women's lib as a pendant on chains around the neck and was made of many different materials and styles. They fell out of style along with the era, although many lesbians still wear them.

I became fascinated with the idea and bought one online, which I still wear. In searching online for a labrys pendent, I came across a magazine of that name published in Atlanta GA. Out of curiosity, I went to it online and found that it largely reported on GLBTOA+ events around the Atlanta area. At the time, I had written three and a half gay stories—the last half still unfinished; I emailed the magazine and asked if they ever published fiction. The editor, Maria Rivers, wrote me back, and said no, but she was a publisher and would be interested in seeing my work. I immediately ran off to Kinko's and made three copies of three finished pieces which I sent to Maria. She emailed me back and said she loved them and that Red Velvet Cape could be made into a movie.

Then as far as I knew, she dropped off the ends of the earth. I spent the next three years trying to get in touch with her again. I tried the magazine and the Atlanta phone directory. Then one day, while playing on the Internet, I checked the Labrys website. It turned out that they had instituted a section where people could write letters to other readers. I wrote immediately and asked if anyone knew how to get in touch with Maria Rivers. I included my phone number and the next morning around ten o'clock, my phone rang. It was Maria. She explained that while on a trip to Mobile, AL some pipes had burst in her apartment. Her computer was trashed, her papers (along with my stories) were a sodden mess and she lost all means of communication with me. She said she had given up the magazine and moved to Charleston, SC. She had been addicted to motorcycles since she was 16 and was now working for Low Country Harley Davidson.

She had taken part in races through the mountains and had taken part in the Myrtle Beach conventions. She was not much over five feet tall and not much over 100 pounds and still was a top rider. We became regular phone pals. She often called me and on speakerphone, while having her dinner, we enjoyed long conversations. On June 6th of that year, while eating her dinner, she told me it was raining. I said, be very careful, you know how slick the painted areas of the street are. I was very aware of the dangers, having ridden a scooter to work and to Sausalito when I was working at the YWCA in San Francisco. She said she was always careful and she was. The guy that turned left (into oncoming traffic at the intersection), and hit her, was not so careful.

Her left foot was nearly severed. Maria spent a long time in surgery, a long time in the hospital, a longer time on crutches, and continued working at Harley Davidson. She had always loved surfing and was determined to get back to it. With unwavering perseverance, she did. To this day, she refers to her left foot as Franken-foot, and wears a slightly different shoe. In the meantime, she gave up the job at Harley and started her own magazine, known as Beau.

It was published in pulp the first year, but since then has been largely online. A few years after the accident, Maria came to California to visit me and to attend the gay pride celebration in San Francisco. When she got out of the car, we looked at each other for about ten seconds. We threw our arms around each other and the bond was set for life. She is my daughter by another mother. From years of aloneness (except for the children) my family was growing.

Shortly before this time, Cassie had returned to Minnesota. She wanted to finish school there and very much missed her tiny niece that she called “mini me.” After a couple of false starts, Cassie began talking about a really great girl she met named Katie. It wasn’t long before she brought her out to visit and we all fell in love with her too. Before long, they were talking of marriage and became engaged. Then came the time when she informed me that she was no longer being called Cassandra, that her name was now Hayden and he was going for gender reassignment. Of all the people I’ve known who have had gender reassignment, this one was a given.

Even when Hayden went by Cassie or Cassandra, she was never known to wear women's clothes, makeup or act in a feminine manner. It was if an ill-fitting shell had cracked and fallen away and the real person inside had at last emerged. Fortunately, Katie remained loving, committed and supportive (which isn't always the case). I consider Hayden my son by another mother.

Milestone 70

During this time, Bink, the Passages psychologist, offered to bring a VA representative to my home who might be able to help me. I was spending far too much time in Enloe with COPD complications. The young woman told me about the local VA clinic and some alternatives to medical help.

She also told me there was money available for someone to help me with low vision equipment and life-skills' training. She agreed to apply for the aid for me and then asked about the broom I have over my door. I explained that I was a pagan and a follower of Yemanja. The young woman got very excited and said that she was a priestess of a pagan group that met periodically at the park. She explained that they were a congregation of an international Druid denomination. Although they called themselves druids, they were all quite eclectic in their practice.

She invited me to the ritual happening the next Sunday and offered to bring me. I agreed; and early Sunday morning they picked me up. The ritual happened to be in a park that was also being used for an annual 6K run that particular Sunday. It made it a little tricky getting in, but we finally managed it.

We met another couple walking in and when we got to the fire circle, there was yet another young woman, Starla, with her four kids bouncing around. The ritual seemed to consist of an introduction, a meditation, the opening of the gates to the other world, an opportunity to make sacrifices of candles, incense, or oil, make requests or give thanks, the closing of the gates, a closing song holding hands, and food. The people were very warm and friendly and reminded me of the hippies in the old days. The meetings usually drew between six and 30 people depending on the weather and the time of year.

The leaders consisted of the young lady who had come to my house, Maeve, her handsome partner, Leneus, the young woman with the kids and seven or eight more regulars. I quickly became a regular and Maeve and Leneus insisted on bringing me to each ritual.

Starla and I hit it off from the beginning. We found we had a ton of things in common and started hanging out together all the time. During this time, we joined the Chico sports club and were going swimming 3 to 5 days a week and I was getting stronger and using the walker less and less. Suddenly, I had a whole new family.

Milestone 71

That was another special blessing because at that point, my health really started to deteriorate. I have to say that I owed the "diversions" of the next few years to cheeseburgers, baked potatoes and Chesterfield cigarettes. When I quit in 1972, they were gleefully announcing that your lungs would heal themselves if you quit. Although the smoking had originated one problem, my current set of issues started with a bellyache at a Yule party. It got so bad when I got home that I finally gave up and called 911.

It was diagnosed as gallbladder trouble and they made me the first patient on the third floor of the new tower at Enloe. The first test proved negative so they decided to do the test a second time. That time, the surgeon in charge decided to take my entire gall bladder out. In the process, he perforated my intestine and in the process of cleaning up, he obviously missed something. Although they never said so, my friends, Maeve, Leneus, Starla, and Bob worried about me all the time.

At one point, when I had stopped breathing, they were about to do a tracheotomy Bob stopped them and said, "Wait." Then he yelled at me, "Attention Marine! Breathe!" Old habits die hard. I started breathing, tried to salute and mumbled Aye, aye. Apparently I did breathe from then on, although some time with help from a ventilator. During this time, Maeve and Leneus kept insisting that when they released me, she and Leneus would take care of me. Because they had messed up the original surgery, I now had an 18" gash in the middle of my belly. Because of this I was on Dilaudid a majority of the time and rarely knew if I was pitching or catching.

During this time, the hospital staff kept telling me that because Maeve was on a cane, she would not be able to care for me. One day, she missed coming to see me; I didn't realize it was her birthday. The hospital staff realized this, took advantage of her absence and convinced me I would be a burden to her. The minute I agreed, they shipped me off to the worst possible nursing home in Chico. I was in a room with a well known dowager who was getting dialysis. She had an ongoing champagne party in her room and her yappy dog was brought to visit daily by her neighbor.

I was so out of it, I hardly minded. I spent most of my time watching the fairies playing in the rainbows on my ceiling or worrying about the old man looking in my window. It rather upset my friends when I begged them to do something about the old man looking in my window. I suppose mostly because there was no old man and they couldn't seem to see my fairies. They began to complain to management because I was not making sense. The management always said it had to do with my age or my meds until my buddy Bob pointed out to them that pus, oozing from my wound was dropping onto my feet.

They said, "what wound?" They were amazed to be pointed to the surgery incision and the pus oozing from under a bandage which hadn't been changed since Enloe Hospital five days earlier. This part is hearsay, but Maeve and Starla swear that when they removed the bottom staple from my incision, pus and infectious material gushed out of me in a prolonged stream 18" high. Starla insists that I was awake and talking, but it's probably fortunate I have no memory of any of this. I was moved to Intensive Care, with some of the nicest nurses on Earth. After a few days they moved me to the second level of care and I could take bed baths—which felt so good.

Using one of my patented smart ass lines (I was feeling better by then) I asked the nurse to marry me, and she said, sure. I gulped and said, I'm not sure we can get married in California, she said (very matter of fact-ly) "I'll find some place." I'm still waiting. During the rest of January and February, that doctor that botched my surgery, tried seven times to put a stent in the gall bladder area. Seven times it failed and they decided to leave the last one and hoped it would work itself out. In March they sent me to Enloe rehab, where wonderful Jamie got me back on my feet in about a month. In April I went to stay with Maeve and Leneus.

At the time, she had a roommate Gordon who had been a CVA and between them, they took such wonderful care of me, she carefully planned nutritious and healing meals for me, and I experienced chia seeds for the first time. Before long, she had me walking up and down the road, and on April 20th, she bought me home to stay.

Milestone 72

My sweet cat princess was so glad I was home; she spent the next few days either on my lap or next to me in bed. I really believe that the loving care I got from my friends, and my cat, and the year and a half I went back and forth to the sports club, are the things that kept me alive. It was a couple years later when COPD hit. I found myself, not unlike a yo-yo, in and out of Enloe every time I couldn't breathe. They would give me intravenous steroids, keep me four-six days and then send me home. After a few months, the routine started again.

It went on for years. In May of 2017, the VA decided to take over. I had one more trip to the hospital after they took over with home health care, and I've had no more hospital trips to this day, a year later. The in-home doctor changed my meds dramatically. I have a nurse who comes once a month to check me out, and a dietitian who encourages me to lose weight. Starla became my care giver when Bob's health would not tolerate it any more. Starla and I try to go swimming as often as possible and I am getting stronger every day.

Epilogue

At 87, fighting COPD (crappy old people's disease) I am blind as a bat, deaf as a post, older than dirt, but cuter than a codfish. And I truly believe that we all should:

"Go through every door, there may be an adventure waiting".

"Never say never unless you are sure that you want something to happen."

"As you sow, so shall you reap—good and bad."

"Don't use your disabilities as excuses; they are blessings that CAN make you strong."

"Add to peoples joys, not their burdens, your reward will be tenfold."

I can hardly wait to see what the next chapter holds for me.

Publishers Note

Sue Handley drew her last breath on the 18th of March, 2019. Sue is survived by her children and leaves behind a legacy of one who rose in a time when lgtbq+ lives were not common place, her bright and sparkling light shines bright in the rainbow of pride that flags the roadway for those that come to discover their true sexuality.

Bibliography

Sue Handley drew her last breath on the 18th of March, 2019. Sue is survived by her children and leaves behind a legacy of one who rose in a time when lgtbq+ lives were not common place, her bright and sparkling light shines bright in the rainbow of pride that flags the roadway for those that come to discover thier true sexuality.

The Three Little Sisters

The Three Little Sisters is an indie publisher that puts authors first. We specalize in the strange and unusual. From titles about pagan and heathen spirituality to traditional fiction we bring books to life.

https://the3littlesisters.com

www.ingramcontent.com/pod-product-compliance
Lightning Source LLC
Chambersburg PA
CBHW070359200726
48294CB00003B/987

* 9 7 8 1 9 5 9 3 5 0 2 9 3 *